ALISSA, PRINCESS OF ARCADIA
by Jillian Ross

Ten-year-old Alissa will one day be queen of Arcadia. That idea excites her. However, she's less excited about the lessons she takes to prepare for her role. Alissa finds herself longing for adventure—and sure she'll never find it.

All that changes when Alissa meets a strange old wizard. Suddenly there's a riddle to be solved and new friends to be made. Best of all, there's a quest to undertake.

Alissa soon finds that her quest is deadly serious. Arcadia is hosting the signing of an important peace treaty. Guests fill the castle—among them an angry knight, a crabby king, and a strange veiled lady. And one of the visitors is secretly plotting to ruin everything. Can Alissa spot the traitor in time to save her kingdom?

STARDUST CLASSICS SERIES

ALISSA

Alissa, Princess of Arcadia

A strange old wizard helps Alissa solve a mysterious riddle and save her kingdom.

Alissa and the Castle Ghost

The princess hunts a ghost as she tries to right a long-ago injustice.

Alissa and the Dungeons of Grimrock

Alissa must free her wizard friend, Balin, when he's captured by an evil sorcerer.

LAUREL

Laurel the Woodfairy

Laurel sets off into the gloomy Great Forest to track a new friend—who may have stolen the woodfairies' most precious possession.

Laurel and the Lost Treasure

In the dangerous Deeps, Laurel and her friends join a secretive dwarf in a hunt for treasure.

Laurel Rescues the Pixies

Laurel tries to save her pixie friends from a forest fire that could destroy their entire village.

KAT

Kat the Time Explorer

Stranded in Victorian England, Kat tries to locate the inventor who can restore her time machine and send her home.

Kat and the Emperor's Gift

In the court of Kublai Khan, Kat comes to the aid of a Mongolian princess who's facing a fearful future.

Kat and the Secrets of the Nile

At an archaeological dig in Egypt of 1892, Kat uncovers a plot to steal historical treasures—and blame an innocent man.

Design and Art Direction by Vernon Thornblad

This book may be purchased in bulk at discounted rates for sales promotions, premiums, fundraising, or educational purposes. For more information, write the Special Sales Department at the address below or call 1-888-809-0608.

Just Pretend, Inc.
Attn: Special Sales Department
One Sundial Avenue, Suite 201
Manchester, NH 03103

Visit us online at www.justpretend.com

ALISSA,
Princess of Arcadia

by Jillian Ross

Illustrations by Nick Backes

Cover Art by Patrick Faricy

Spot Illustrations by Katherine Salentine

Stardust
CLASSICS

Just Pretend, Inc.
Attn: Publishing Division
One Sundial Avenue, Suite 201
Manchester, NH 03103

Stardust Classics is a registered trademark
of Just Pretend, Inc.

Second Edition
Printed in Hong Kong
04 03 02 01 00 99   10 9 8 7 6 5 4 3

Publisher's Cataloging-in-Publication
(Provided by Quality Books, Inc.)

Ross, Jillian.
　　Alissa, princess of Arcadia / by Jillian Ross; illustrations by Nick
　　Backes; spot illustrations by Katherine Salentine. -- 2nd ed.
　　p. cm. -- (Stardust classics. Alissa; #1)

　　SUMMARY: Ten-year-old Princess Alissa must study deportment
　　to learn to be a proper queen, but her secret studies with a wizard
　　enable her to avert disaster at a ceremony of alliance with
　　neighboring kingdoms.

　　Preassigned LCCN: 97-73130
　　ISBN: 1-889514-03-9 (hardcover)
　　ISBN: 1-889514-04-7 (pbk.)

　　1. Princesses--Juvenile fiction. 2. Wizards--Juvenile fiction.
　　I. Backes, Nick. II. Salentine, Katherine. III. Title. IV. Series.

PZ7.R67Ala 1998　　　　　　　　[Fic]
　　　　　　　　　　　　　　　　　QBI98-684

Contents

CHAPTER ONE

A Proper Princess

 dmund, this simply cannot go on any longer! Something must be done."

"Yes, something!"

Princess Alissa inched closer to the archway outside the great hall of the castle. She could hear her great-aunts Matilda and Maude easily. But the gentler voice of her father, King Edmund, was just a murmur from where she stood.

Alissa knew that it was wrong to be listening. Her great-aunts had scolded her about it many times. But after all, Alissa was the one about whom "something must be done." And she wanted to know what that something was going to be.

"The princess is impatient," said Great-aunt Matilda.

"Impatient," echoed Great-aunt Maude.

"Her manners are poor. Her deportment is terrible," Matilda continued.

"Terrible," added Maude.

Alissa sighed. Even if she could hear her father, it looked like he wasn't going to get a word in.

Drat birthdays! Alissa thought. Since she'd turned ten, just two weeks ago, her life had changed. And very much for the worse. For as long as Alissa could remember, she'd been free to wander the castle grounds. She could climb haystacks,

1

visit the kitchen—even ride with the young pages.

But since her birthday, all she'd heard was talk about good manners and ladylike behavior. And about how lacking she was in both. Now she was expected to turn into a proper princess. To her great-aunts, that meant sitting without wiggling, embroidering without knots, and reading poetry without giggling.

The sound of footsteps brought Alissa back to the present. She stood up straight and tried to look like she'd just arrived at the spot.

"Can I be of any help, your majesty?" asked a chilly voice.

Alissa turned to see the tall, bony figure of Sir Drear, the king's steward.

"Ummm, no thank you," she said. "I was just, I mean…"

Sir Drear smiled a weak, gray sort of smile and bowed. "Then I'll take you to your father, your majesty," he said. "I know he has been waiting for you." He motioned the princess forward.

Alissa took a deep breath and walked through the archway. She paused to study her father. But Alissa couldn't read anything from his calm, kind face.

Her great-aunts were another matter. They were looking quite satisfied. Tall, skinny Matilda wore a thin-lipped smile. Plump, rosy Maude beamed her usual silly grin.

"Alissa!" cried Great-aunt Matilda. "My dear, we were just talking about you."

"Yes," fluttered Great-aunt Maude, the echo. "We were."

"Come in, Alissa," said her father. He turned to the great-aunts. "Alissa and I need to talk for a while," he said. The two old ladies nodded and swept out of the room.

Then the king glanced at Sir Drear, who still stood nearby.

"Alone," he added.

"Of course, your majesty. I will be outside, waiting for your command." Sir Drear bowed a deep bow and backed out of the room.

Alissa sat down on a long bench. She looked fondly at her father. How royal he seemed, even with his beard wild and uncombed. Just like Alissa's own dark brown hair, which never stayed in place.

"You're very quiet, Alissa," said the king as he sat beside her. "That's not like you. Surely you must wonder what we were talking about."

Alissa glanced up. Did he know that she'd been listening?

"Oh, Father," she whispered. "You're not going to send me away to learn to be a lady, are you?"

"Send you away?" he said. "Where did you get that idea?"

"Cook said a serving maid said a page said he heard the great-aunts talking about it," answered Alissa.

"What have I told you about listening to wild stories, Alissa?" warned her father. But his dark eyes gleamed with kindness. He added, "Of course I'm not going to send you away. I promised your mother that long ago. And have you forgotten how much having you here means to me?"

"I haven't forgotten, Father," Alissa said softly.

Alissa had never really known her mother, Queen Elizabeth. The queen had died when Alissa was just a baby.

But Edmund often talked of his wife. Elizabeth had been patient, thoughtful, and wise. Exactly as a queen should be. Exactly as Alissa feared *she* would never be. She looked down sadly at her clasped hands.

The king drew her to him. "Alissa, you know that someday you'll be queen of Arcadia," he began.

"Yes, I know," she answered. She leaned her head on his shoulder.

"Well, there are certain things expected of a queen," her father went on. "And your great-aunts are right. I haven't made sure that you've learned all you need to know. Maybe if your mother were here to teach you..." He trailed off sadly.

"Oh, Father," Alissa cried. "You've taught me everything I need to know. I've been watching you. You're a wonderful king."

"You can't learn all you need to know just by watching me," replied her father. "You're very lucky to have your great-aunts here to teach you."

Alissa wrinkled her nose. "Lucky? Why do I have to learn how to fold a handkerchief? Or what sauce goes with which meat? Or how to hang a tapestry? None of that is important."

"Alissa, the matter is decided," said King Edmund in a firm voice. "Tomorrow you're to start deportment lessons with your great-aunts. They will help you learn the proper manners you'll need someday as queen. And later you'll work with Sir Drear. He'll teach you about Arcadia's history and about how to run the kingdom."

Alissa groaned. "But when will I have time to ride? Or visit the dogs in the stables? Or practice my archery?"

The king gripped his daughter's hands. "Alissa, preparing to be a queen means accepting responsibilities."

Alissa bowed her head, but King Edmund gently raised her chin. "That doesn't mean you don't have any freedom. I agree that you should have time for your own interests. So in the afternoons, you may choose your lessons. Riding, archery, chess—whatever you wish. Just be sure to pick a teacher with the knowledge and patience you need.

"And Alissa," he went on. "About your deportment lessons. There are some things you need to learn quickly." He suddenly looked very serious.

"What do I need to learn?" Alissa asked. "And why?" The idea of learning quickly appealed to her. Though she couldn't picture Matilda and Maude teaching anything at more than a snail's pace.

The king answered her with a question. "You know that Arcadia will be hosting the Ceremony of Alliance soon?"

Alissa nodded. There'd been talk of little else in the castle. There was to be a banquet, followed by a ceremony. At that ceremony, many kings and queens would sign a treaty, promising to protect one another. The agreement would keep the kingdoms safe from their enemies. Especially from Cirrus, a powerful kingdom to the north.

"I know, Father," she said. "Cook has been getting ready for days. And everyone has been talking of the jesters and minstrels and kings and queens who are coming and—"

King Edmund held up his hand, and Alissa fell silent. "There's far more to the ceremony than food and fun, Alissa. And you need to understand, because you'll be part of it."

Alissa was shocked. "Me?" she asked. Up till now, she'd only watched royal ceremonies.

"Why?" she asked in excitement.

"Roderick, king of Thalia, will be here. He's agreed to sign the treaty," said her father. "Do you understand what that means to Arcadia?"

Alissa answered at once, "Of course." Then she added slowly, "Well, no—not really. I mean, I know Thalia is very powerful."

"That's true," agreed King Edmund. "Yet there's something even more important. It's been years since Thalia last signed a treaty with another kingdom. With them as part of the alliance, we'll be strong enough to stand up to Cirrus."

"But why am *I* to be there?" asked Alissa.

"Because you're now old enough to take your place at my side," King Edmund replied. "And because having you there will be a sign to Roderick of my trust."

He gave Alissa a fond smile. "After all, everyone knows that you're the most precious thing to me in all of Arcadia."

The king became serious again. "I must warn you about something. King Roderick is said to be fussy and easily upset. You have to know how to behave and not bring dishonor to us. Otherwise, there may be no alliance."

Alissa started to sputter, "Father, I'd never—"

Then she stopped. She remembered some past dinners. A frog that suddenly hopped out of a serving dish. A lord and lady's quiet talk interrupted by a fit of giggles. A bossy knight who found his gloves tied in a knot. No, she hadn't always done things in exactly the proper way.

"I understand, Father," Alissa said quietly. "And I'll do my best to make you proud."

"I know you will," said King Edmund. "Now go and talk to your great-aunts. They'll tell you when to report for your lessons."

Alissa left the great hall and slowly walked up the steps. My life is over, she thought. If only I were nine again!

But then Alissa remembered her father's words. She was to be part of the upcoming ceremony. Little bubbles of excitement rose in her stomach.

Maybe being ten wasn't all bad. Not if you got to do really important things.

⌇

Halfway through the next morning, Alissa had changed her mind again. Her first deportment lesson wasn't going well. And she'd decided that being part of a ceremony wasn't enough to make *this* worthwhile. No matter how important the ceremony might be.

"Alissa!" A sharp voice broke into her thoughts. She'd been studying a sunbeam that was trapped in the great-aunts' gloomy chambers. Trapped, thought Alissa. Just as I am.

"I am waiting for your answer," said Matilda.

"I'm sorry, Great-aunt," said Alissa. "I didn't hear the question."

"She asked about the Thalian custom for toasts," said Maude helpfully.

"Toasts?" repeated Alissa. "Ummm…"

"Yes, toasts," snapped Great-aunt Matilda. "Come now, you must remember. I told you that first the king makes his toast. Everyone except the king drinks. Then, while the Thalian king raises his cup, all others lower theirs. And the king drinks alone. It's really quite simple."

"Yes, I remember," sighed Alissa.

"Just be sure you remember during the ceremony," said Matilda.

Alissa frowned. There was so much to learn! How to walk. How to curtsy. How to rise from the table. She'd never remember it all.

But she had to. She couldn't let her father down.

Alissa was able to control her impatience for the next

hour. Finally her great-aunts excused her for the day. Quickly she headed for the warmth of the castle kitchen.

Alissa found that the kitchen was the usual mix of mess and activity she so loved. And ruling over all was Cook.

Cook was a big woman. As big and solid as the huge cuts of beef she roasted on outdoor spits. And her voice was as loud as a bull's bellow. But roar though she might, Cook was really soft and gentle.

Cook saw Alissa at once. "My, my!" she exclaimed. "I thought you were much too old to be hanging around here anymore." Yet her eyes gave her away. It was plain that she'd missed Alissa as much as Alissa had missed her.

"Do you know what a bother it is being ten?" cried Alissa. "All morning I've been stuffed with manners and customs. Customs and manners. And the great-aunts go on and on, saying the same things over and over. I can't bear it!"

"Enough of that," said Cook. "The dear old ladies mean well. And after all, they're your father's own aunts. You must show some respect."

Cook turned back to her stew. But she kept on talking—as if she were speaking to her big black cooking pot.

"The king's a good man," she said. "A wise one too. But I fear he's let you spend too much time with the likes of me."

"Oh, Cook, no! That's not true! I love you."

"And I you," said Cook matter-of-factly. "But I'll not have you talk about your great-aunts in such a way."

9

Cook poured something hot and spicy into a wooden bowl. "Now sit here and taste this." She put the bowl down in front of the princess.

Alissa took a sip. "It's wonderful!" she said. "What is it?"

"Eel stew," replied Cook. "I want to fix something special for the banquet."

"The banquet," Alissa moaned. "At least you know what you're supposed to do. And how to do it. But I'm afraid I'll never be a proper princess. At least not in time for the ceremony."

"There, there, lamb," said Cook. "You can do it. Haven't I always said that you have a will of iron? Just set your mind to anything, and it's yours. That's what I've always said. It won't hurt you to learn a bit of patience from the old aunts either."

With that, Cook turned back to her work.

For a while, Alissa sat and listened as Cook chatted with the butcher and beekeeper. What they had to say was much more interesting than her great-aunts' dull talk.

Alissa sighed once more. She was sure that she'd never become the kind of princess she was expected to be.

At supper that evening, Alissa sat with Great-aunt Matilda. How she missed the days of eating in the kitchen under Cook's less-than-watchful eye.

"Wipe your spoon," scolded Matilda. "And remember, you are the younger. That means you must cut the meat."

Alissa sighed again—it seemed that she'd been sighing all day. She picked up her knife and speared a chunk of meat from the serving bowl. Then she placed the meat on the bread trencher and sliced carefully. Finally she passed the whole thing to her great-aunt.

As for herself, Alissa could only nibble some of Cook's fresh-baked bread. She wasn't very hungry tonight.

Alissa didn't think she could sit still for another moment. When a visiting minstrel began playing his lute, she only half listened. So often minstrels sang on and on about some knight's love for his lady.

But tonight was different. Alissa found herself caught up in a tale of a brave knight who went questing.

As Alissa listened, she couldn't help but wish that she were in the knight's place. How exciting to just get on one's horse and head out into the unknown! No responsibilities. No boring banquets.

The thought of going on a quest seemed wonderful. But it was hopeless. Alissa was a princess. And she'd never heard a minstrel sing of a princess going on a quest. At least not a proper princess.

CHAPTER TWO

The First Riddle

After dinner Alissa quietly slipped out of the castle. She decided to head for her father's private gardens. She often went there when she wanted time just to think.

As Alissa stepped onto the path, she found the ground wet under her feet. "Witches' warts!" she cried. "The great-aunts will have my head for coming out here in my indoor slippers."

Alissa sat down on a bench and removed the soggy slippers. Then, using only her toes, she picked up stones. One by one, she dropped them into the pool nearby.

Plunk. Plunk. Plunk. "Good evening."

Alissa jumped up off the bench and spun around. Behind her stood an old man cloaked in a glittering robe.

"Who are you?" she asked, trying to keep her voice steady. "And what are you doing here? Don't you know that these are the king's private gardens?"

The old man slowly moved closer. Then without so much as a by-your-leave, he sat on the bench.

"So they are," said the old man. His voice sounded like the creaking of a rusty old hinge. "And where better to find a princess? For it's you I've come to talk to."

"To me?" said Alissa. "I don't mean to be rude, good sir.

But why should I talk to you?"

"Perhaps for the same reason that you want to go on a quest," replied the stranger.

Alissa was startled. How did he know she'd been thinking about a quest? She'd never said anything about it to anyone. She hadn't even really thought about such a thing until tonight.

She stared at the old man in wonder. Deep wrinkles lined his face, like an apple left too long in the barrel. His white, wispy hair snaked in and out of his collar. A full beard flowed almost to his waist. And his strange, glittering cloak puffed and billowed, even though there was no wind.

"Now sit back down," ordered the old man.

Alissa found herself strangely willing to obey. So she sat.

For several heartbeats, there was silence. Then the old man spoke.

"Yes, I know about your wish for a quest. And about your poor manners. And about your lack of patience. I know all about you."

"But, but—" Alissa began.

"And I decided it was time for us to meet," he said. "Don't you agree?"

Alissa leapt to her feet again. "No, I certainly do NOT agree!" she stormed. "And who are you to talk to me in this way? Surely you know that princesses are not to be spoken to in such a manner!"

"Not usually," agreed the old man. "But then you're not exactly the usual princess, are you?"

Alissa couldn't argue with that. Slowly she sat back down.

"Yes, Alissa, I know a good many things about you," said the old man. He gave a dry chuckle. "For instance, I know

that you worry about your new responsibilities. And I think…"

Here he leaned closer and peered nearsightedly at the princess. Then he reached into a deep pocket hidden under his beard. He pulled out a pair of golden spectacles. Placing them carefully at the end of his long nose, he studied her again.

"Just as I thought. You are not content. You are searching for something."

Alissa felt as though a great weight had been lifted from her shoulders. She stared at the old man. "You're right," she said. "I'm not content, but I don't know why. And I do worry about my responsibilities. And," she admitted with a shrug, "I am rude and impatient—sometimes. But how do you know all this about me? I've never even seen you before."

The old man closed his eyes for a moment. "Perhaps you have never seen me. But that doesn't mean that I've never seen you."

He opened his eyes and rose to his feet. "We will meet again, princess," he said.

"When? And how?" cried Alissa. Suddenly she realized that she wanted to see—had to see—this strange old man again. "And who are you? Where will I find you?"

"Ah," murmured the old man as he combed his fingers through his beard. "All good questions, Alissa. And perhaps a search for the answers should be your first quest."

"My first quest!" exclaimed Alissa. "Am I really to have a quest?"

"We shall see," said the old man. "We shall see. It all depends on you. But you'll need some help. So let this be your guide."

The old man drew himself up. He looked taller and younger—and much more powerful. In ringing tones, he said:

> Unwind this riddle to its end
> If you will seek this strange old man:
> Find me where today becomes tomorrow,
> Yet yesterdays still linger;
> Where neither ground nor air is master,
> In a shelter cloaked in danger.

As soon as he finished speaking, the old man turned to go. Alissa jumped up to follow. She cried out, "Wait! Please wait! What's that supposed to mean?"

But as she started forward, Alissa slipped on the wet ground. By the time she righted herself, all she could see was a swirl of mist. The old man had disappeared into the dark shadows.

"How could he have moved so quickly?" she asked. "Who is he? And what exactly does his riddle mean?" But she received no answers from the empty garden.

Saying the strange words to herself, Alissa headed back inside. Within moments only her wet slippers remained to mark the meeting.

CHAPTER THREE

The Quest Begins

That night Alissa tossed and turned in her bed. Over and over, she repeated the old man's riddle.

"*Where today becomes tomorrow,*" she said to herself. "Why, that makes no sense! How can today ever be tomorrow?"

Alissa thumped her pillow three times. It didn't help. She couldn't sleep. And she couldn't solve the riddle.

Finally Alissa threw off her coverlet. She drew aside the heavy bed curtains and got out of bed. Then, pulling a robe over her shoulders, she went to the window.

Alissa loved the way the castle looked on a night like this. The watchtowers glowed in the moonlight. The gardens below cast deep, sleepy shadows.

"I'll never figure out the meaning of his silly riddle," Alissa whispered to herself. "And I'll never get to go on a quest." She leaned her forehead against the stone wall. "I wonder where I would have ended up if I'd solved the riddle?"

The soft moonlight calmed Alissa, and she shut her eyes. It seemed that she rested for only a moment. But when she opened her eyes again, the moon was high overhead. Before long the first hints of dawn would brighten the sky.

"That's it!" she cried. "The answer is right in front of me! *Where today becomes tomorrow*—that has to be the east.

Tomorrow comes with the sunrise. So he's somewhere facing east. Or to the east. Or both! But what can he mean by *yesterdays still linger?* And where could he be that *neither ground nor air is master?*"

Alissa stared at the eastern sky, trying to understand the old man's words. Then her eyes lit upon a tower—a tall tower that rose in the east. It stood in the farthest, oldest part of the castle.

"*Yesterdays,*" she whispered. "The past! That tower is the oldest thing in the kingdom. And *neither ground nor air is master.* A tower sticks up in the air, yet rises from the ground! It has to be the old tower!"

Without stopping to figure out the rest of the riddle, Alissa threw on her clothes. Then she grabbed a candlestick from her nightstand.

Alissa took a deep breath and opened her bedchamber door. She crept past the king's quarters, the great-aunts' chambers, and down the cold stone steps.

At last she reached the kitchen. Safe! No one would be up for some time.

But as Alissa hurried through the room, she heard a rustling noise behind one of the storeroom doors. A mouse? One of the castle dogs?

The door creaked open. A figure darted forward.

Alissa screamed and grabbed one of Cook's frying pans. The dark figure screamed back, and the princess almost dropped the pan in fright.

But the stranger didn't move again. So Alissa stopped to take a good look. To her surprise, she saw that it was only a girl! A girl just about her own age. The hood of a rough cloak covered her red hair. And in her hands, she held a cloth sack.

"Your majesty," the girl breathed. Then she curtsied. It was plain that she knew who Alissa was. And Alissa thought she might have seen the girl before, though she couldn't put a name to the face.

Alissa's courage returned. "Just what are you doing?" she asked in a low voice.

The girl drew herself up proudly and looked right at Alissa. "I was stealing some food," she announced.

Alissa was surprised at the girl's honesty.

"For heaven's sake, why?" asked the princess. "You know that stealing food from the king is a crime."

"I do," said the girl. "But so is living a life of misery. And that's what I'm doing."

"What does misery have to do with food?" Alissa asked. "My father sees to it that no one goes hungry in his kingdom."

"You wouldn't know, milady," said the girl. "Seeing as how you're a princess and all." Then she threw down her bag and planted her hands on her hips. "So just call the guards and get it over with. I'll take my punishment."

"Don't be silly," hissed Alissa. "I'm not going to call the guards. Anyway, what did you think you were going to do once you took the food?"

"I was going to run away," said the girl. "I've been a serving maid to Lady Matilda this whole week. I've found it's not a position that suits me."

"So that's why you look familiar," Alissa said. "And now I can understand why you're running away."

"And you, milady? Why might you be running away?" The girl motioned toward the princess's cloak and candle.

Alissa frowned. "I'm not running away." Then she

announced proudly, "I'm on a quest."

"A quest," said the girl. "I guess that's all fine and good for nobles. For those with time for such foolishness."

Alissa was hurt. "Quests are not foolishness!" she said, forgetting to keep her voice down. Her words echoed off the walls.

She lowered her voice at once. "And they're not just for the nobility," she said. "Anyone can go on a quest."

Alissa stopped to think about what she'd just said. Anyone could go on a quest—even a runaway. Especially one who seemed brave and honest. Besides, Alissa would welcome some company. Questing was much scarier than she'd thought it would be.

Alissa grinned. "In fact," she said, "why don't you join me? After all, you can't run away now that I've discovered you, can you?" She waited hopefully.

"Well, milady, I don't know," said the girl. "How far might you be going?"

"I'll explain everything," promised Alissa. "But first tell me your name."

"It's Lia, milady. Daughter of Joseph the baker and Bess the weaver."

"Follow me, Lia," said the princess. "And I'll tell you all about my quest." She headed for the door at the far end of the kitchen.

Lia waited for a moment. Then she shrugged and fell into step beside Alissa.

As she led the way across the courtyard, the princess talked steadily. She explained about the old man, his riddle, and how she'd cleverly figured things out. By the time she finished, the girls were at the foot of the old tower.

"Are you sure we should be doing this, your majesty?" asked Lia. "Haven't you heard the stories about this tower?"

"What stories?" Alissa paused to ask. To be honest, she was in no real hurry to open the door.

"There are those that say the tower is haunted," whispered Lia. "Sometimes strange lights can be seen. And shadows."

Alissa shivered. Now the last part of the riddle was starting to make sense. At least the *danger* part.

"I don't care," Alissa said. "I must find the old man if I want to have a quest. And I'm sure he's in this tower. So stay here if you want, but I'm going up."

Alissa pulled on the iron handle. At first the door refused to move. But finally it swung open with a loud creak. Alissa stepped inside, with Lia right on her heels.

The girls stopped when they caught sight of a long stone stairway. The steps seemed to curve up and up without end. Damp moss covered the walls, while cobwebs hung overhead. Everything smelled stale and stuffy.

"Let's go," said Alissa, sounding braver than she felt. She started up the steps.

"I don't know, milady," said Lia. "It looks like no one has been here in a very long time. And it's so dark. Surely it can't be safe to climb up all that way."

"It's a quest, Lia," Alissa argued. "Quests aren't supposed to be safe."

Lia sighed. "I wish I'd known that before I agreed to come along."

Alissa paid no attention. She was counting steps to keep from thinking about what might lie just ahead. "31, 32, 33..." she said. "34, 35—"

A thunderous crash rolled toward them from above. The

number *36* died in Alissa's throat. She threw her arms around Lia, almost knocking her down the stairs. The two clung to one another in fear.

When no other noises were heard, the girls crept upward again. Around the next bend, they found a suit of armor. It lay in a heap on the narrow landing.

Lia burst out laughing. "It's just some rusty old armor!"

Alissa angrily kicked at the heap of metal. "What's it doing here?" she muttered. "And why did it fall now?"

Again the girls started up the steps. They continued to climb for what seemed like hours. Once, when a bat dived toward them, Lia wanted to run back to the bottom. But Alissa forced her onward. And when they reached a curtain of thick cobwebs, even Alissa thought about giving up. But this time, Lia went forward. She brushed the cobwebs aside and wiped her hand on her skirt.

At last the stairs stopped twisting and turning. The girls had reached the final landing. There before them was a great wooden door.

In silence they studied the heavy door. From its center rose an enormous knocker in the shape of a fearsome dragon's head. And beneath it shone a thin line of light.

Alissa stood frozen in place. It was Lia who finally said, "May as well get it over with. Seeing as how we've come this far."

Alissa raised her hand to the knocker. But as she did so, the door swung open.

CHAPTER FOUR

The Wizard's Tower

lissa stepped back. She couldn't go far because Lia was hiding right behind her.

"Welcome, princess." Framed in the open doorway was the strange old man from the garden. "And you, too, Mistress Lia," he added.

"Mercy!" whispered Lia. "How does he know my name?"

The old man chuckled. "I know many things, both useful and useless. I count your name among the useful things," he said with a bow. "Come in, ladies."

Remembering her brave words about questing, Alissa led the way into the tower room.

Once inside, the two girls stood and stared in wonder. Running down the center of the room was a long wooden table. Dozens of bottles cluttered its surface. Not far from the table, a huge fireplace was set into one wall. A bright, snapping fire burned there. Over the flames hung a steaming black pot.

In front of a window stood another table. A large crystal ball sat on its surface. The ball glowed with a strange colored light. Nearby a huge book resting on a tall stand also seemed to shine faintly.

Between the many windows hung thick tapestries covered with stars, suns, and moons. Here and there, doors peeked through gaps in the tapestries. Alissa found this extremely strange. How could there be doors in the walls of the tower? Where would they go?

"Congratulations, princess," the old man said as he walked back to his pot. He added a handful of yellow powder, and flames shot up. "I see you've successfully begun your quest by solving my riddle. And by braving a few dangers to find me here."

Alissa at last felt her powers of speech return. "I guess I have," she said. Slowly she moved to stand in front of the old man. "So now, sir, will you please tell me who you are? And why you're here?"

"I am Balin—a wizard," he announced. He spoke as calmly as if he were claiming to be a mere blacksmith or beekeeper. "And I've lived in this tower far longer than you've been alive."

"Oh, me," gasped Lia. "A wizard!"

But Alissa wasn't satisfied. "How can that be?" she questioned. "I've lived here all my life, and I've never seen or heard of you."

"That's right, Alissa," said the wizard. "The time for us to meet had not yet come. Now it has."

"Does my father know you're in this tower?" Alissa asked.

"He did once. But I suppose he's long since forgotten me," muttered Balin.

He waved this aside and went on. "However, that doesn't matter. The tower is mine for as long as I wish it. The right to it was given to me by your father's father's father. It's become my *shelter,* if you will. In case you were still struggling with the last part of your riddle," he added.

"Just how old are you then, sir?" asked Alissa.

The wizard tipped his head back to consider. "I don't think your arithmetic skills are quite ready for that, Alissa," he said. Then he clapped his hands. "Now that you're finally here, we must get started."

"What do you mean?" asked Alissa.

"It's time to begin your lessons," stated the wizard.

"Lessons!" groaned Alissa. "Please don't tell me you're going to teach me deportment as well," she begged.

Balin smiled. "Never fear. My powers are not that great. I'll leave your deportment to the great-aunts. No, I'm speaking of lessons in wisdom and magic."

Magic! Alissa was shocked. She'd never dared dream of learning anything so exciting.

"Will I learn spells?" she asked. "Like how to make myself invisible? How to open locked doors without keys? How to turn Squire Hubert into a frog?"

"You may," said Balin. "But I trust you'll also learn to use your powers wisely. That means not wasting them on young bullies like Hubert." He fixed his steely eyes on Alissa. "If I didn't think you had promise, I wouldn't have chosen you as a student."

Then the wizard turned to Lia. "And what about you, Lia? Are you interested in magic as well?"

"Me, sir?" asked Lia in surprise. She thought about the question for a minute. Then she smiled shyly. "To be honest, sir, I think not. Magic frightens me."

The wizard nodded. "It can be frightening, Lia. Learn if you will—and what you will. In any case, you're welcome to keep the princess company here whenever you choose."

Then, with a grand sweep of his robe, Balin rose to his full height. "Now," he said, "let's begin."

Alissa waited, hardly breathing. What would her first lesson be? Something truly magnificent, she hoped.

Two colorful feather dusters magically appeared in Balin's hands. He gave one to Alissa and the other to Lia. "Attack the cobwebs, ladies. And be sure you don't break anything."

"Dusting!" sputtered Alissa. "That's my first lesson? I am NOT a maid!"

"No," Balin coolly agreed. "A maid would have better manners."

"What's dusting supposed to teach me?" Alissa shot back.

"So you think dusting is not a useful skill?" asked the wizard. "Do you know how to dust? Do you know what you'll learn from dusting?"

Alissa bit her lip. Then she mumbled, "No. To all three."

Balin nodded. "Well, then…dust!"

"Wait a minute," Alissa said. "What about Lia? I'm sure she's dusted before. What could she possibly get out of this?"

"Ah," the wizard said. "Perhaps the satisfaction of giving a princess a highly useful lesson."

Lia laughed. "That's a good enough reason for me," she said. She moved over to the table and began dusting.

"Hmmmph," Alissa snorted. She was beaten—for now. She picked up her feather duster. Watching Lia and carefully copying every move, she set about dusting. "Bother this!" she whispered now and again.

However, the princess soon became wrapped up in her task. There were so many wonderful things in the wizard's tower. Hundreds of books (all in need of dusting!) with strange pictures, maps, and words. How many places Balin must have gone to have collected so many different books! Alissa longed to read every one.

She also dusted bottle after bottle full of liquids and powders. And others that didn't seem to hold anything at all. Most were labeled. Alissa recognized several names, though their uses were new to her. She studied a jar of garlic. Someone had written, "Good for head colds." Alissa would have to tell Cook about that.

As Alissa moved to the huge book on the stand, the duster fell to her side. She stared open-mouthed at the book, which was turned to a picture of a dragon. Or at least it seemed to be a picture. Alissa cried out when she saw the green-and-gold beast flick its tail.

She jumped back, slamming the book shut. A huge cloud of dust flew up.

"What's the matter?" the wizard called.

Alissa coughed and sneezed. "That book!" she choked out.

"Yes?" the wizard asked.

Alissa stamped her foot. "You know very well what I mean!" she cried. "The book is magic, isn't it?"

"All in good time," Balin said.

The princess stamped her foot again. "In good time?" she exclaimed. "But magic is what interests me. Not dusting! I hate dusting! I'm terrible at it. I can't do it!" She threw the feather duster on the floor.

The duster gave a loud squawk and ruffled its feathers. In a twinkling, the duster had become a parrot—a very noisy parrot.

"Can't do it! Can't do it!" repeated the parrot in loud squawks.

"Enough, Bartok," said the wizard mildly. The parrot flapped its wings and flew to an iron bar that hung overhead.

"Glory be," whispered Lia.

"Now *that's* real magic!" said Alissa.

Balin sighed. "Yes—though of a very common sort."

"Common! It seems wonderful to me. That's just the kind of thing I want to learn," declared Alissa.

Balin pulled at his beard. "Alissa, you may have thought your dusting was a meaningless task. But ask yourself some questions about your first lesson. What did you see as you dusted? What did you observe about me? What treasures did you find? And how much more might you have discovered if you'd shown a little patience?"

The wizard flicked some dust off his robe. "Well, that's enough for now. You must get back before anyone finds that you're missing."

"And why is that?" asked Alissa in a quiet voice. She felt a bit silly about her show of temper.

"Because no one is to know of your visits to this tower," the wizard replied. "Magic is filled with secrets, Alissa. Not everyone can be trusted with them."

Alissa paused before answering. "I won't lie to my father. If he asks me about you, I'll have to tell him."

"You're free to do so," said the wizard. "As I trust you, so I trust him."

Alissa thought over the wizard's words. Then she nodded. She asked Balin if she could come to the tower in the afternoons. She explained that her father had given her that time for lessons of her own choosing.

The wizard agreed. Then he turned to Lia. "And what of you?" he asked. "Will you be returning with Alissa?"

Lia turned to the princess. "I'm not really free to come, milady."

"Ah, yes. We haven't solved this running-away problem," said Balin.

Lia gave the wizard a surprised glance. "You knew I was running away?"

But Alissa was getting used to the wizard by now. She merely looked thoughtful. Then she made a decision.

"I think I might know how to deal with that!" she said. She turned to Lia. "Would you be willing to stay and be my lady-in-waiting?"

Lia's eyes grew huge with wonder. "Why, milady, I'm a serving girl. A lady-in-waiting must be of noble birth."

"You're noble enough for me," announced Alissa. "So let's go talk to Great-aunt Matilda."

"Lady Matilda will be more than happy to see the last of me," Lia sighed. "However, I don't think she'll like this idea."

But Balin nodded at Alissa. "You've made a wise decision. Now you must fight for it."

He turned back to his table, acting as if the girls were no longer there. They tiptoed out of the room. As Alissa pulled the door shut behind them, they heard Bartok's farewell:

"Can't do it! Can't do it!"

"Horrible bird," muttered Alissa as she started down the stairs. "I liked him better as a feather duster."

Lia sighed. "He's right, though. You can't do this. Just let me get on my way. I'll be gone before Lady Matilda thinks to look for me. Please, milady."

"Oh, don't be foolish," said Alissa crossly. She turned to look at Lia, who stood on the step above her. "And stop this 'milady' silliness, will you? Call me Alissa."

For a moment, the two girls just stared at one another. Then they both smiled.

Alissa went on in a quieter voice. "You know, there are some things a princess can't get just by asking. Friendship, for example." She looked up at Lia with a question in her eyes. "We haven't known each other long. But I'm already sure that I'd like you to be my friend."

"It's done, milady," said Lia softly.

"Lia!"

"I mean, it's done, princess…I mean, Alissa. But, glory be, I can't call you by name in front of anyone. It would mean my hide."

"All right," Alissa gave in. "But will you call me by name when it's just us?"

"I will…Alissa," said Lia.

Alissa reached out her hand and Lia took it. Holding hands, the two girls finished their trip to the bottom of the tower. Then softly they crept back inside the castle.

～

After breakfast Alissa reported to her great-aunts for deportment lessons. For once she paid great attention. But she couldn't help watching Lia. Her friend was struggling to unwind some yarn that Great-aunt Maude had tangled.

"Well, Alissa," said Great-aunt Matilda as they finished up. "I must say that you've shown real progress. It appears that our lessons are beginning to have a positive effect."

"Most positive," murmured Great-aunt Maude. Her eyes were also on Lia, who was still struggling with the yarn.

"Oh yes, Great-aunts," said Alissa, with her hands held together in a ladylike manner. "And I've been thinking. If I am to be a proper princess, it's time I had a lady-in-waiting."

"Hmmm," said Matilda. "You may be right, Alissa. You are too old for a nursemaid now. So you should have a lady-in-waiting. Someone soft-spoken and gentle. Someone who can school you even more in the skills of a lady. Let's see—"

Great-aunt Maude broke in. "I believe Sir Drear has a niece who just might do."

"Actually, Great-aunts," began Alissa, "I've already picked someone."

"What?" asked Matilda.

"What?" echoed Maude.

"Yes," Alissa went on. "I've asked Lia to be my lady-in-waiting."

Matilda twirled around. Her flashing gray eyes lit upon Lia, who was trying to make herself invisible.

"Lia!" Matilda cried. "Why, she's a peasant! A serving girl! And her work isn't entirely satisfactory, I might add!"

Alissa hurried to Lia's side. "Lia is everything a lady-in-waiting should be. She's thoughtful, brave, truthful. And she knows how to dust!"

Lia stood and curtsied to Matilda. "Milady," she began, "forgive the princess. She means well—"

"Forgive?" screeched Matilda. She grabbed Alissa by the hand. "We shall see what the king has to say about this

32

foolishness."

Matilda stormed out of the chamber, dragging the princess behind her. Alissa in turn took hold of Lia and pulled her along.

Last came Great-aunt Maude, clutching a tangled ball of yarn in one hand. Gently she muttered, "Foolishness. Yes, foolishness."

CHAPTER FIVE

The Magic of Words

atilda moved at what Alissa felt was an unlady-like speed. At the entrance to the great hall, Matilda plowed right past a waiting servant. "I will announce myself!" she hissed. Then she dropped Alissa's hand and marched right up to the throne. Alissa, Lia, and Maude trailed along after her.

"Edmund!" Matilda barked.

King Edmund had been talking to Sir Drear. Now both he and his steward looked up in surprise.

"Lady Matilda!" Sir Drear cried. "Whatever is going on? Have I forgotten that you have an appointment with his majesty?"

"Appointment," snorted Matilda. "Appointment, indeed."

"It's all right, Drear," the king said. Then he turned to Matilda. "Is something troubling you?" he asked calmly.

"Troubling me?" asked Matilda in a shaking voice. "Troubling me?" Maude remained silent. Matilda was doing her own echoing today.

"I should say so," Matilda went on. She grabbed Lia by the arm and pushed her toward the throne.

"This, sire, THIS is who your daughter considers a suitable lady-in-waiting."

Sir Drear gasped. But the king's face remained thoughtful

and calm. Lia stared back at him just as calmly.

Alissa rushed forward to explain. However, the king held up his hand to silence her. Then he spoke gently to Lia. "What's your name, child?"

"I am Lia, your majesty," she said. "And you should know that I'm not a fine lady. I'm the daughter of Joseph the baker and Bess the weaver. So you see, Lady Matilda is right. I'm not fit to be a lady-in-waiting. I haven't even been a good serving maid, sire." She bowed her head.

The king studied Lia. Then he looked at his daughter's worried face. For a long moment, there was silence in the great hall.

At last King Edmund got to his feet and stepped down closer to the girls.

"Lia," he said, "you know that my daughter can be stubborn and impatient?"

Lia paused. "I have heard it said so, sire," she admitted at last. She went on quickly, "But I also know that she's kind and brave."

King Edmund smiled. Then he said, "I agree that it's time the princess had a lady-in-waiting. Someone of her own choosing." He placed a hand on Lia's shoulder. "And I think you will be both a loyal companion and a true friend, Lia."

Alissa threw her arms around her father. "Oh, Father," she cried, "you'll see. With Lia to help me, I'll be the most proper princess anyone has ever seen!"

Great-aunt Matilda was thunderstruck. "Edmund!" she cried.

"Matilda," said the king, "I've made my decision. Please be sure that Lia joins the princess for all her lessons. Including her deportment lessons."

Alissa curtsied to her father. Lia did the same. Then, leaving Matilda sputtering behind them, the two girls turned and headed out of the great hall. Alissa walked like a proper princess. And Lia walked beside her, like a proper lady-in-waiting. But when they reached the hallway outside, they both burst into giggles.

"Come on, Lia," gasped Alissa when she was able to talk. "We have to get your bedchamber ready. You can have the chamber right outside my room. And we must have a dress made for you."

The girls raced up the stairs, forgetting to act ladylike in their excitement.

~

That afternoon Alissa headed back to the tower alone. Lia had decided that becoming a lady-in-waiting was enough excitement for now. But she promised to help Alissa learn whatever the wizard taught.

This time the trip up the tower steps seemed to go much faster. Before long Alissa was knocking on the great door.

"Begone! Begone!" squawked Bartok. Alissa pushed open the door anyway.

"Welcome," said Balin. "Good afternoon to you, princess. And congratulations again—this time on your new lady-in-waiting."

"How did you know?" asked Alissa. "I was going to tell you all about it."

Balin motioned toward his glittering crystal ball. "I watched here," he said.

Alissa walked over to the crystal. She lifted one hand, but the wizard quickly ordered, "Don't touch that!" Alissa jumped back.

"I just wanted to look inside," she said. "Can you see everything that goes on? Is it real magic?"

"Real?" repeated the wizard. "Well, its dangers are real. At least for those who don't know how to use it. Now let's get started."

And so began the day's work. But it was too much like the dusting lessons for Alissa's taste. The wizard asked her to wash, dry, and polish every one of his bottles. All that after she'd just dusted them!

"Surely there can't be another bottle in the whole kingdom," said Alissa as she finished. "At least I hope not."

Then she spun around. "If you really are a wizard," she asked, "why must I wash these bottles? Why can't you just wave your hand and make them shine?"

"One thing you must learn, Alissa, is that magic cannot do all things. No matter how powerful it is. And even when it can be used, it must be used wisely and well."

He pointed to the bottles. "That means not using magic simply to save oneself work."

"Of course," sighed Alissa. "That's what you have a helper like me for."

The wizard just smiled. "Come, Alissa," he commanded. He motioned toward a carpet near his great book stand. "Be seated."

"Are we to practice some magic now?" asked Alissa as she sat down.

"Soon, soon. You have much to master first," said Balin. "Before the practice of magic comes the practice of wisdom."

"No magic?" said Alissa sadly.

The wizard tapped his foot. "A *little* magic," he replied.

"Remember, Alissa…patience."

Balin cleared his throat. "To begin with, we'll learn about healing. Common herbs and spells to ease the troubled mind…"

Alissa listened closely for some time. But hard work and lack of sleep caught up with her. Before long she found her eyelids getting heavy.

"And what words would you use, princess?"

Alissa jerked awake to find Balin staring at her. "Words? For what?" she asked.

The wizard's eyes darkened. "You must learn these words. And many others. For that is where the power of magic truly lies. If used properly, words can turn sorrow to joy, injustice to justice."

Alissa said softly, "I'll try."

"Very well," said Balin. "Here's something to help you begin." He handed Alissa two books from the shelf along the wall. "Memorize these," he ordered.

"Memorize both?" asked Alissa.

"Everything worth learning requires work," said the wizard. "Now we're done for today," he announced.

As Alissa started down the stairs, she cracked open one of the books. "No dragons this time," she whispered to herself. She didn't know whether to be glad or disappointed.

～

The next few days passed quickly. The princess made time at night or just before dawn to read the wizard's books aloud. And after listening to Alissa read, Lia asked question upon question.

Soon Alissa's head was filled with a number of spells and potions. And words—a great many words. She was sure she would never keep them all straight.

Mornings were still spent with the great-aunts. Alissa was so tired that it was easy to sit quietly and act like a lady. Maude and Matilda were pleased. "It appears that Lia is good for Alissa after all," Matilda actually said one day.

Most afternoons were spent in the wizard's tower. There Alissa ground herbs and roots to make medicines. She learned some simple spells. She even found time to scrub the wizard's black pot until it shone.

Sometimes Lia went along with the princess. More often Alissa went alone. But at night, the two girls always talked about Balin's lesson for that day.

One evening toward the end of the week, the king appeared at Alissa's door.

"Good evening, Alissa," Edmund said. "And good evening to you too, Lia."

"Father!" cried Alissa, putting down her book. "What a nice surprise! Nothing's the matter, is it?" she asked. Her father didn't usually visit after she'd gone to her chambers for the night.

"I wanted to talk with you, Alissa," the king said. "First, I wished to say how pleased I am by your progress. Your great-aunts say you've been doing well."

"Thank you," said Alissa. "I've been trying."

"I know," replied the king. "And I know it's hard to spend time on matters that don't interest you."

He sat next to Alissa. "I was wondering whether you've decided how

39

you'll spend your afternoons?"

"I think I have," Alissa answered.

"Excellent," said King Edmund. "And are you happy with your teacher?"

Alissa thought for a moment. "Yes," she replied. "Though I'm not sure he's always happy with me."

The king chuckled. Alissa thought he might ask what she was studying. But instead he paused. His smile turned into a worried look. Finally he said, "Alissa, I have a favor to ask."

"Of course," said the princess.

"I'd like you to be King Roderick's dinner partner at the banquet," said her father.

"Dinner partner? To King Roderick?" repeated Alissa in a shocked voice.

King Edmund nodded. "I know it's a great deal to ask," he said. "But we have no queen in Arcadia. So it would be fitting for you to do so. And we could show him no greater honor."

Alissa twisted her hands. "Oh, Father, I don't think I can manage such a thing! I know I'll make some horrible mistake and ruin the banquet for you."

"I wouldn't ask if it weren't very important," said her father. "And I know you can do it." He leaned over and dropped a kiss on his daughter's head.

"I've spoken about this to your great-aunts. They'll see to it that you learn all you need to know," he said. With a good-bye to Lia, the king left.

"Dragon's dewlaps," muttered Alissa. "Lia, I must learn magic as fast as possible. Nothing else will get me through this banquet!"

CHAPTER SIX

A Message in the Crystal

The next morning, Alissa and Lia arrived early at the great-aunts' chambers.

"Well," sniffed Matilda. "It's good to see you so interested in your lessons."

"Very good," echoed Maude.

Alissa swallowed her pride. "Please, Great-aunts, I need your help," she said. "Father told me last night that I'm to be King Roderick's dinner partner. I'll never be able to get through the banquet without ruining everything!"

"Don't be silly, my dear," said Matilda. "With us as your teachers, you will be able to handle anything. Even King Roderick."

That morning Alissa hung on every word from her great-aunts. She even asked for more.

"And if the king wants a second serving of meat?" she questioned.

"As the younger, you must serve him," said Matilda. "But never dip his meat in the salt dish. Take some salt between your fingers. Then sprinkle it on the meat."

"Sprinkle, don't dip," echoed Maude.

Alissa was still repeating rules as she left the great-aunts' chambers. "Don't leave the spoon in the serving dish. Elbows off the table. Wipe the cup before passing it to the king. Oh,

Lia, I can't remember all this!"

"You're doing fine, Alissa," said Lia. But in her heart, she was worried for the princess.

Downstairs the girls found almost everyone busy with chores. Servants were polishing the silver, beating dusty rugs, and sweeping away cobwebs. Meanwhile, footmen spread fresh rushes on the floor.

Alissa watched the work with sympathy. I know how tired they must be, she thought. Until now she'd never realized how hard it was to keep a castle clean.

Sir Drear was busy directing the work. "No!" he called to a young page. "You have that tapestry upside down!"

"I'm sorry, sir," said the boy. "It looks the same either way to me."

Alissa smiled. "If it weren't for worrying about the dinner, this would be fun. Come on. Let's go and see Cook." Alissa always felt better after a visit to the warm kitchen.

When they arrived, serving maids were rushing back and forth. Cook was in the middle of the activity, making a fancy castle from sugar. "For the final banquet," she explained with a smile. She offered a taste of the sugar to Alissa and Lia.

"Did you hear?" asked Alissa as she licked the last sweet grains from the spoon. "I'm to be King Roderick's partner at dinner."

Cook chuckled. "I did hear that," she said. "And I'm sure the king will find it a banquet to remember." Then she noticed

Alissa's sad face. "There now," she added quickly. "I only meant that he'll find you a treat."

Alissa sighed. "I don't know," she said. "I think he might enjoy your sugar castle more."

"Not true, my lamb," Cook said. She caught Alissa up in a hug. "Things will work out," she whispered gruffly. "You'll see."

From the kitchen, the two girls wandered into the great hall. Visitors from kingdoms near and far were beginning to crowd the castle. A feeling of excitement filled the air.

Suddenly a trumpet sounded outside. "Another king or queen must be arriving!" cried Alissa. "Let's watch!"

The girls hurried to the window to find a long line of people nearing the castle. Some were on foot, while others rode. In front were a trumpeter and squires with banners. Next followed the performers—jugglers, minstrels, and jesters. Then came the fine ladies, their dresses covered by traveling cloaks.

Finally the knights appeared. And just in front of them rode a big, red-bearded man. "That must be their king," said Alissa.

The trumpeter sounded one last call. Then Sir Drear stepped out into the courtyard. In a voice loud enough to be heard by half the kingdom, he gave his greeting. "On behalf of Edmund, king of Arcadia, you are welcome, King Roderick."

"King Roderick!" Alissa gasped. So here was her dinner partner!

The king of Thalia swung down from his horse. Quickly a groom ran forward to take the reins. Roderick took a few steps. Suddenly he stopped. He glanced at the ground and frowned. Then he turned on his heel and marched back to his knights.

A puzzled Sir Drear looked at the ground as a Thalian squire ran toward him. Alissa heard Drear ask, "Is something wrong?"

"The king refuses to walk across the dusty courtyard without a carpet," said the boy.

Drear stared for a moment longer. Then he called a page, who soon returned with a carpet. With the blast of a trumpet, the carpet was unrolled. At last Roderick stepped forward and entered the castle.

"Did you see that?" moaned Alissa. "I'll never be able to act properly enough for *this* king!"

She turned and headed back to the great-aunts' chambers. "Come, Lia," she said. "I need more lessons today."

Later, as she headed up to the wizard's tower, Alissa was still fretting about the banquet. "There must be a spell he can show me," she said to herself. "Something that will keep me from making an awful mistake."

Alissa rapped on the tower door and hurried inside. She barely took time to greet Balin before sharing her troubles. In a rush, she told him about fussy King Roderick and her part at the dinner.

Alissa ended by begging, "Please, Balin. I need your help. Can you teach me a powerful spell? One that will keep me from doing something wrong at the banquet?"

Balin shook his head. "Come, Alissa. Have you forgotten what I told you? Magic must be used wisely. And you're not ready to learn powerful spells. There are other things you should master first. Remember, everything must be learned in order. So let's begin."

He went to his huge book and began flipping pages. "Ah, here we are," he said. "Reading the future from the warts of a toad…"

Alissa found that idea interesting. She moved to Balin's side and began to read over his shoulder.

The lesson soon came to an end. Alissa still had no magic to see her safely through the banquet. But she did have two new spells to practice. Maybe she really could learn to read the future! Then she'd know if she was going to make a mistake. If she found that she was, she could talk Balin into giving her a spell. Or just leave Arcadia before she ruined the alliance.

At the bottom of the tower, Alissa found Lia waiting for her. "Alissa," Lia said in excitement. "You must come and see! The entertainers from Thalia are practicing!"

At Lia's words, Alissa forgot about spells. Lia led the princess to the courtyard. Alissa gasped in delight as she took in the scene. Acrobats were tumbling. A minstrel was playing his lute. And a jester and magician were doing tricks.

"Look at that," Alissa pointed. The magician had lit a torch and was now putting it in his mouth.

"That's not a trick I care to learn," said Lia.

Alissa's eyes moved to the colorful jester. The bells on his cap jingled merrily. And as he danced past, sparks of light flew from his shoes.

"How does he do that?" asked Alissa.

"I don't know," Lia said. "Perhaps the wizard could explain it to you."

That night at dinner, more entertainers put on a show. By the time Alissa visited Balin the next day, she was full of questions. She told him about the sights she'd seen. "Oh, Balin!"

she exclaimed. "I want to learn to do magic like theirs!"

The wizard sniffed. "What you see are merely tricks. Hocus-pocus. Not real magic."

"But what about the jester who makes sparks with his feet?" asked Alissa.

"Pooh," said Balin. "Give me your slippers, princess."

Alissa handed her shoes to the wizard, who placed them on a table. He opened a bottle of brown liquid. Carefully he dripped a little liquid onto the soles. Then he waved the shoes in the air.

"A magical spell?" Alissa asked.

"No. I'm drying them," said Balin. He looked at the shoes once more. "Now it's time to make sparks fly."

He handed the slippers to Alissa. "Put them on," he ordered. While she did so, Balin moved the rugs that covered the stone floor. "For the moment, forget about walking like a princess. Run like a jester."

Alissa darted across the floor. To her delight, sparks shot out whenever her feet touched the stone!

"How does it work?" asked Alissa when she tired of making sparks. The wizard went into a long explanation of rare metals.

"So you see, much of what appears magical is only knowledge of the unusual," said Balin. "What's important is that you learn the difference."

He went on. "Now let's find out if you can tell the future. It's time to try the spells I gave you yesterday."

He walked over to his crystal ball and sat on the stool

nearby. "I'll check my crystal to see if you're right," he said.

Alissa began the lesson. But things didn't go as well as she had hoped.

First the princess took a toad from a bag she'd tied at her waist. She placed the animal on her palm and studied its back. However, she couldn't read a thing from its warts.

"I think it's too frightened to show me the future," Alissa finally said. She explained, "I took the poor thing to bed with me last night. He looked so cold. But this morning, I found that he'd hopped into Great-aunt Maude's bed."

She went on to tell him that Maude's screams had awakened the whole castle. And Alissa had barely saved the toad from a broom handle.

She was surprised when Balin said nothing. Instead, he stared at his crystal ball for a time. Then he waved her on. "Try the next spell," he said.

This time Alissa was sure she'd be able to read the future. She held four small sticks in her hand to warm them. Then she repeated the words Balin had taught her. "Sticks of boxwood, sticks of ash, show your truths to me." She threw the sticks down on the floor.

Balin's eyes remained on the crystal while Alissa studied the jumbled sticks. At last she gave up. "I can't read anything in them," she said sadly. "I forgot that the sticks must be dropped, not thrown."

Alissa fought back tears. "I'll never be good at this," she moaned. "And I'll never get through the ceremony without making a mistake!"

She looked to Balin for comfort. But the wizard was still staring into the crystal. The look on his face made her forget her own worries.

"Balin," said Alissa. But the wizard didn't answer.

Alissa crossed the room. When she gently touched the wizard's sleeve, he jumped.

"Balin, are you all right?" asked Alissa.

At first Balin just continued to stare at the crystal. When he raised his head, Alissa was shocked by what she saw. His dark eyes were filled with fear.

"Disaster!" exclaimed the wizard. "The crystal shows only disaster!

CHAPTER SEVEN

A Mouse in the Corner

isaster!" Alissa repeated. "What do you mean? What do you see?"

Balin turned back to the crystal. "I see lies and treachery. A danger to the alliance. And if this comes to pass, Arcadia will be at war!"

"War!" cried Alissa. "Quickly, Balin. Look again. Does the crystal tell you what we can do?"

The wizard shook his head and frowned even more deeply. "For some reason, I can't read the crystal clearly. All I see are mere hints. A few words. Such a thing has never happened to me before."

"Oh, Balin, try again," she begged. "I'm sure you can read the crystal if you just look closer."

Balin carefully lifted the crystal ball from the table. For a long time, he stared in silence.

At last he sighed and put the crystal down. "It's hopeless," he announced. He rose and began to pace back and forth across the tower. "Now even the little bits I saw earlier are gone," he said.

"Is it possible that you're forgetting something? Some magic words maybe?" asked Alissa. She thought it unlikely. Still, forgetting things certainly kept *her* from doing magic well.

"No," said the wizard slowly. "I haven't forgotten anything.

But perhaps someone—or something—is blocking me. If I'm able to…"

Suddenly he raised his arms over his head. "Cumulus, nimbus, stratus!" he chanted.

Alissa watched open-mouthed as rain began to fall from the tower ceiling.

The wizard lowered his arms, and the rain stopped. The water droplets on the floor steamed and then vanished.

"Yes," he said, "that's it. My powers are still present. But someone is blocking the crystal."

Now Alissa was really frightened. "Who, Balin? And what are you going to do? You must save Arcadia!"

Balin stared thoughtfully at her. "I am not all-powerful, Alissa. Perhaps it is *you* who will do something. Maybe this is the quest you were seeking."

"But I haven't even done a single spell right!" Alissa moaned.

Balin took Alissa's chin in his hand and raised her eyes to his. "Have you already forgotten what I've taught you? Magic may not be the answer to this problem."

Alissa said nothing. Magic might not be the answer, she thought. But a really strong spell certainly couldn't hurt.

Balin continued. "Do you remember what I told you about words and their power?"

Alissa nodded. " 'The power of magic is in the words,'" she repeated.

"The only weapon we're being

51

given is the words in the crystal," the wizard said. "And those aren't clear. So we must treat them like a riddle and seek their meaning."

"Like a riddle?" she asked. "What do you mean?"

"You solved a riddle to find me," said Balin. "And you did so by using your powers of thought and observation. Perhaps you can use those same powers to solve this puzzle."

"Why can't I just warn my father?" asked Alissa. "Then he and his soldiers can fight off this danger."

Balin shook his head. "No. While I can't read the crystal clearly, I can see this much. It's not in the king's power to prevent this treachery. In fact, if he were to try to do so, I foresee an even greater disaster."

"But how can that be?" cried Alissa.

"I don't know," said the wizard. "There are mighty powers at work here. Just who or what controls them, I can't tell. These powers have woven their web very tightly. But they haven't taken you into account."

"Balin, I just don't understand what you want me to do," said Alissa. "Or how I can save Arcadia."

"Come, princess," said the wizard. He motioned toward a stool. "Sit, and I'll tell you my plan."

Alissa sat and listened.

"Whoever is blocking my magic knows about me and my powers," Balin began. "So if I appear, I'll be able to do nothing. Our enemy will be ready for me—masked, hidden, invisible. But you, Alissa—you can be a mouse in the corner."

Alissa frowned. A mouse? He wants me to be a mouse? She wasn't sure she liked being compared to such a common animal.

"Yes, a mouse," said Balin, reading Alissa's thoughts once

again. "A mouse that hides in the corner and says nothing. You belong in the court, Alissa. No one will think anything of your presence there."

He continued. "But unlike a mouse, you'll use your mind and powers of observation. Watch and listen. Then come to me with what you discover. And bring things that belong to those you suspect. I can then use my magic to read their thoughts. Do this, Alissa, and together we'll solve the riddle."

The wizard finished and looked at Alissa hopefully.

"I'll do it," she said slowly. "But I'll need help."

"I will always be here," Balin promised her. "And count on Lia to be a second set of eyes and ears." Then he stared at Alissa. "Watch for the unexpected," he said. "And remember that things are not always what they seem to be."

"I'll remember," said Alissa. She got down from the stool and headed for the door.

"Alissa," called Balin. "You're forgetting something."

"I am?" said Alissa as she turned to look at the wizard. "What?"

"The words you need," he said. "The bits of words I was able to see in the crystal." He stepped closer. "Think about the meaning of this: *Ever present, yet invisible.*"

"*Ever present, yet invisible,*" Alissa repeated as she opened the door. She was thinking so hard that she never heard Bartok's usual squawk, "Begone."

CHAPTER EIGHT

The Veiled Lady

lissa rushed back to her chambers to find Lia.

A single glance told Lia that the princess was upset. At once she jumped to her feet. "Alissa!" she exclaimed. "What's the matter?"

"Something terrible is going to happen!" Alissa replied. She quickly told Lia about the crystal and its message of coming disaster.

"Such a strange clue," said Lia. *"Ever present, yet invisible.* How can something be both present and invisible?"

Alissa thought for several moments. "The air around us is present, yet invisible. But I can't see any danger in the air."

"Unless it means that a storm is coming," said Lia.

"It must be more than that," sighed Alissa. "The wizard spoke of treachery. And that means we must look for a person. But who? And how will we know?"

"Well," suggested Lia, "we can start by watching everyone at dinner. It's time we went down anyway."

"Let's go," said Alissa.

The two girls hurried to the great hall. They found the room already filled with people. Guests sat at the long tables, stood in small groups, or wandered about the room. Servants rushed back and forth with heaping platters of fish and meat. Meanwhile, the castle dogs searched under the tables for bones and scraps.

The princess looked around. Her father and King Roderick were seated at one end of the hall. Edmund was leaning toward Roderick, listening carefully. The Thalian king frowned as he spoke.

"He's probably complaining again," said Alissa. "Thank the stars that I don't have to eat at his table today. The sight of that frown would make me lose my appetite."

The girls found a spot in a far corner of the great hall. A serving boy brought water to them, and they washed their hands. Then they began to eat. But their thoughts were on the words in the crystal rather than their food.

Midway through the meal, a bald-headed nobleman staggered by. He held a goblet in one unsteady hand.

Alissa wrinkled her nose as the noble passed. A thoughtful look came over her face. She jumped to her feet and grabbed a page by the arm. "Do you know who that is?" she asked, pointing at the bald man.

"That's Lord Gilbert, my lady," said the page.

"Ah!" said the princess. While the page watched and scratched his head, Alissa began to follow the lord. Lia quickly rose and ran to catch up with her.

"Alissa," she hissed. "What are you doing?"

"Did you get a whiff of that noble?" asked Alissa.

"It would have been hard not to," answered Lia. "He smells like he traveled here in the company of pigs. What of it?"

"Don't you see?" said Alissa. "*Ever present, yet invisible.* You can't see his smell, but it certainly is present. He just might be the one who's the traitor."

"I'm not sure that smelling bad means he's the one," said Lia.

"Well, you can't be sure he isn't," said Alissa. "So I'm going to follow him."

"Fine, then," sighed Lia. "I'll come along."

So Lord Gilbert soon had two shadows. But he never noticed that he was being followed. He had more important things on his mind—such as filling his stomach. Whenever servants passed by, he helped himself to their platters and jugs.

"How sickening!" said Alissa. "*He* should be the one who has to have deportment lessons."

Finally she turned to Lia. "This lord could never come up with a plan," she said. "He's all belly and no brains!"

Alissa spun around to head back to their table. Ahead of her, she saw Sir Drear talking to a lady dressed in red. Alissa started to turn to avoid the steward and the lady. Then she stopped and stared.

"Lia," she whispered. "Look at that lady!"

Lia stared too. The lady in question was tall and thin. But not unusually so. What *was* unusual was the veil that completely covered her face. Her features were a blur behind the cloth.

"That veil," said Alissa. "I wonder why she hides her face. Perhaps she's not really who she says? And think about it, Lia. *Ever present*—the veil. *Yet invisible*—we can't see her face. This time I'm sure I've solved the riddle."

Alissa started after the veiled lady. "Now where are we going?" asked Lia.

"I'm going to keep an eye on her," replied Alissa. "And maybe you can find out who she claims to be."

Lia looked doubtful. But she headed off in the opposite direction anyway. In just a few minutes, she was back.

"She's Lady Gwynne from Pellinore," Lia reported. "And I

discovered more. She's staying in the small chamber next to your great-aunts' room. That's because she refused to share a room with someone from Thalia!"

"Then she must be an enemy of Thalia," Alissa said. "Did anyone say anything about the veil?"

Lia shook her head. "No, but I'll see what I can find out."

The princess watched Lady Gwynne for a while longer. However, she learned nothing more. The lady spoke to few people. And she never lifted her veil.

Alissa glanced around but couldn't spot Lia. So she decided to carry out her next idea alone.

Quietly she stole from the hall and up to the sleeping chambers. She needed to find something the wizard could use to read the lady's thoughts.

No one was in sight as Alissa walked down the hall. Quickly she darted into the small chamber the lady was using during her stay in Arcadia.

In the dim light, Alissa noticed an open chest against the wall. She knelt next to it and began searching through the lady's belongings. Her hand touched something soft. "This will do!" whispered Alissa as she pulled out a glove. "It's not like I'm stealing it," she added. "I'll bring it back."

Alissa tucked the glove into her sleeve and slipped out of the room. But as she headed down the hall, she heard footsteps. Was a lady-in-waiting returning? Or Lady Gwynne herself? There was no time to hide!

When Lia rounded the corner, Alissa breathed more easily. "Lia," she whispered. "Come with me!"

Alissa hurried Lia to their chambers. There she pulled the glove out of her sleeve.

"This belongs to Lady Gwynne," said Alissa. "That means

it can be used to read her thoughts."

"Are you going to take it to the wizard?" asked Lia.

"Well, I was," Alissa said slowly. "But I'd better not go now with so many people about. I think I'll just try to read it myself."

Alissa dropped to her knees and pulled a heavy book from under her bed. "I'm sure I can find a suitable spell in here," she said.

"Maybe you should wait until you can take the glove to Balin," warned Lia.

"Wait?" said Alissa. "We don't have time to wait!"

Yet several hours later, Alissa was still waiting. She'd found spells for reading someone's belongings. But since she lacked a few ingredients, she'd had to make changes.

"I don't understand," she muttered. "I can't get any idea of Lady Gwynne's thoughts from this glove."

"Perhaps that's because you used beeswax instead of honey," said Lia.

"Well, it should work," said Alissa. "Both come from bees."

"Maybe it's time to take the glove to Balin," suggested Lia. "I'm sure the halls are quieter now."

"You're right," sighed Alissa. "Besides, he's the wizard. *He* should be doing this work, not me."

She tucked the glove into a bag she wore at her waist. Then she put on her cloak and sneaked out into the hall. By slipping from shadow to shadow, she avoided those guests who were still up. At last she reached the wizard's door.

"Balin!" Alissa cried as she burst into his chamber. "I've solved the riddle!"

"Really?" said Balin. "I'm delighted. And surprised. That required less thought than I imagined. Well, let's hear your observations, princess."

Alissa quickly told the wizard what she had learned. Then she pulled out the glove. "Here's the proof," she said, handing it to Balin.

Balin took the glove and let it hang from two fingers. "Hmmm," he said. "It's certainly proof that Lady Gwynne's servants don't take care of her things."

Alissa blushed. "Well, I'm afraid I'm to blame for the stains," she admitted. "It's beeswax," she added.

"Beeswax," repeated Balin. "Pray tell, how did you get beeswax on the lady's glove?"

Alissa's eyes dropped to her lap. "I...I tried a spell," she said slowly. Then she looked up and went on. "I couldn't get here while all the guests were about. And it was late. And I wanted to *know*," she finished in a high, rushed voice.

"I see," said Balin. "How did you know which spell to use?"

"I didn't," she said softly. "So I just tried a few."

Balin sighed. "Alissa, have you forgotten what I told you about patience?"

Alissa threw up her hands. "I didn't forget, Balin. I just couldn't wait. This was too important!"

Balin shook his head. "The more important the matter, the more important it is to be patient."

Then Balin stood. "Enough. Let's see what the glove tells *me*." For several minutes, he remained motionless, glove in hand and eyes closed. Finally he sighed and sat down heavily.

"There is no evil in this lady," he announced.

"How can you tell?" asked Alissa. "You didn't even do a spell."

"No," replied Balin. "I just turned my mind to the lady and her thoughts," he said. "Not all magic is showy and exciting."

Balin rose and moved to his crystal. "Now let's satisfy your curiosity about the veil," he said. "Then we can leave this lady in peace."

"But I thought you couldn't read the crystal," Alissa objected.

"Some things are blocked from my sight. But not all," Balin said. He stared into the crystal ball for a long time. Alissa saw a look of deep sadness come over his face.

"Balin," she cried. "She is evil after all, isn't she? That's why you're so sad!"

"You're jumping to conclusions, Alissa—again!" said the wizard crossly. "No, she isn't evil. The crystal shows me that she's badly scarred from an illness. One that almost took her life. She wears the veil to protect herself from the pitying eyes of others. So you can understand why she wouldn't want to share a bedchamber—with anyone."

He stared at the princess for several long moments. Finally Alissa's eyes dropped. "I didn't know," she whispered.

"Remember what I've told you, Alissa," said the wizard.

"You mean about being patient?" she sighed.

Balin smiled. "Well, that too. But also remember that things are not always as they seem to be. The one we seek is clever. He or she will not be easy to find. So don't look for the easy answer, Alissa. Take time to think things out."

"Can you read anything more in the crystal?" Alissa said. "Anything that might help me?"

"Only more hints of words," replied the wizard. "Another piece to the riddle."

"What words this time?" Alissa asked.

The wizard closed his eyes and said: *"Unmatched power, but little respect."*

"What does that mean?" cried Alissa. "This riddle is getting even foggier."

"I don't understand it either," said Balin. "So you must go back to your observing and thinking."

As Alissa got ready to leave, Balin handed the glove to her. The princess scratched once more at the beeswax. "Can you do some magic to clean Lady Gwynne's glove?" she begged. "I hate to return it to her like this."

The wizard smiled. "You already possess the necessary magic."

"I do?" asked Alissa. "What is it?"

"Soapwort," he answered. "And lots of rubbing to make suds. Now good night, Alissa."

CHAPTER NINE

The Dark Knight

ore words!" cried Alissa the next morning. She was telling Lia about her visit to the wizard. "That's all I have. More strange words. But I know even less than before."

She went on. "I was so sure Lady Gwynne was the traitor. But I was wrong—again." Alissa picked up the lady's glove. "At least I got this glove clean. Finally!"

She tossed the glove under her bed. "I'll return it later," she sighed. "Right now we have more important things to do. We'd better get started."

The two girls headed downstairs. "Thank goodness there are no lessons today," said Lia.

Alissa nodded. "That means we have all day to finish this quest."

The great hall was as crowded as it had been the evening before. Some guests were just stirring from the floor mats on which they'd slept. Others had already started on the day's activities. In spite of her worries, Alissa was fascinated by all that was going on.

"Look at that!" she said to Lia as they passed two jugglers. They were laughing and throwing knives back and forth.

"And that!" cried Lia. She pointed to an acrobat who was walking on her hands.

The girls stepped around a minstrel. He looked up but kept right on playing a merry tune on his lute.

They smiled as they passed the Thalian jester. He was following Sir Drear, copying the steward's stiff walk.

"No one here looks the least bit like a traitor," said Alissa. "Anyway, I see the great-aunts heading our way. Let's go out to the stables before they corner us."

Lia followed Alissa into the courtyard and down to the stables. There they found more people and activity. Grooms and stable boys were whistling and shouting as they did their chores. Horses snorted and stamped as the girls passed by.

Suddenly they heard an angry voice. "Stop!"

Alissa pulled Lia behind a huge post. From there they watched as a knight dressed all in black approached a stable boy. The boy was about to put a bucket of feed before a magnificent white horse. The huge man jerked the boy away from the stall.

"My horse doesn't eat this slop!" he shouted. "I told you that when I arrived!"

"Yes, milord," stammered the boy. "I mean, no, milord. I mean, I forgot, milord."

The knight gave the boy an evil look. "See to it that you remember from now on," he said. Then he charged out of the stable, nearly knocking down a page as he went.

"Now there's a villain if ever there was one," whispered Alissa. "I'm going to keep an eye on him."

"I'll see what the stable boys know about him," offered Lia. She headed toward the back of the stables.

Meanwhile, Alissa trailed behind the knight. She tried to

look as though she were just out for a walk.

Near the gatehouse, the knight stopped. In front of him stood two knights from Thalia.

"Let us pass!" said one of the Thalians.

The dark knight growled, "Brave words from a coward."

The Thalian knight reached for his sword. But his friend stopped him. "Come! Don't waste your time on this fool!"

The huge knight laughed and walked away. The two Thalians stared after him with looks of hatred.

Alissa remembered the last words Balin had read in the crystal: *Unmatched power, but little respect.*

He's powerful, she thought. And the Thalians certainly don't respect him. In fact, they treat him like an enemy. And that means he must be an enemy of the alliance.

Though sure she was right, Alissa tried to be patient. Besides, she still needed to take something of the knight's back to Balin.

The princess slipped along the edge of the courtyard, keeping the knight in sight. She didn't see a wooden bucket that stood in her way. With a loud crash, the bucket went flying across the courtyard. The knight whirled around, one hand on his sword.

"Are you following me, girl?" he barked.

"N-n-no, sir," stammered Alissa.

The knight frowned at Alissa for a moment. Then he turned and stormed off. The princess watched, but this time she didn't follow. Instead, she turned and made her way back to the stables.

Alissa found Lia waiting by the stable door. "Did you learn anything?" she asked.

"A little. The knight's name is Sir Damon," Lia replied.

"He's said to be powerful and daring."

"Well, listen to this," said the princess. She told Lia about the Thalians and their hatred of Sir Damon. "So I'm sure we've found the villain," she finished. "Now if only I had something to take to the wizard."

"What about a piece of the knight's horse blanket?" asked Lia. She pulled a dirty, tattered scrap of cloth from her sleeve. "I took it while the stable boy wasn't looking."

"I don't know whether that will work," replied Alissa. "But let's get it to Balin and find out."

"You go," said Lia. "I'll see if I can find out anything else."

Alissa gave her friend a grateful look and hurried off to the tower.

By the time Alissa reached the wizard, she was out of breath. She placed the cloth in Balin's hands. He wrinkled his nose. "Phew!" he said. "What is this?"

"It's a piece of horse blanket," Alissa said.

"I might have guessed," muttered the wizard.

"Will it tell you anything about the knight who owns the horse?"

"Perhaps," replied Balin. "But first I need to know what you've found out about him."

So Alissa told the wizard what she and Lia had learned. "He is powerful," she concluded. "And he isn't respected—at least not by the Thalians."

Balin stood with the cloth in his hands, his eyes closed. Then he sighed and handed it back to Alissa.

"What did you learn?" she asked in excitement.

"You are right," the wizard began. Then he held up his hand, "But only partly right. The knight is powerful. Yet he's not a danger to the alliance."

He moved to his crystal and looked inside.

"What does the crystal tell you?" Alissa asked. "I can't believe it shows anything good about him!"

"Some bad," Balin admitted. "The Thalians say Sir Damon cheated at a joust. That's why he hates them, and they him."

Then Balin shook his head. "Yet I find no sign that he's a friend of Cirrus. He's here because he hates Cirrus even more than he hates Thalia."

"He seems like such a villain," Alissa said sadly.

The wizard turned back to the crystal. "Let me see if I can read anything else."

Balin stared into the glassy ball. "There are more words here," he said at last. "But they are even fainter than those I saw before." Slowly he repeated the words aloud: *"Outside the same, yet inside different."*

Alissa groaned. "All these riddles! Are they each separate? Or parts of the same riddle?"

"I can't be certain," Balin said. "But I think this is like a puzzle. All the pieces must fit together to make a whole."

He put a hand on Alissa's shoulder. "I don't know how to make these pieces fit, Alissa. However, I think you can do it."

Alissa's lips quivered. Though she didn't say anything, her mind was filled with doubts.

～

That afternoon Alissa and Lia wandered around the castle grounds. They talked about the knight and the new words in the crystal ball.

"Two of the acrobats we saw this morning looked like twins. That means they're the same outside," said Lia. "Could it be them?"

"I don't know!" groaned Alissa. "Do the words mean two people? Or do they mean two things? This is impossible!"

At dinner that evening, Alissa continued to look for clues. She studied the guests closely as they watched the acrobats, minstrels, and jesters. But she discovered nothing new.

Alissa grew quieter and quieter.

The jester passed by. When he saw the princess, he came to a sudden stop. He frowned a huge frown. Next he touched the corners of his mouth and stretched his lips into a smile. But Alissa didn't smile in return.

The jester jingled the bells on his cap and wiggled his fingers. Then he reached out and pulled a golden coin from behind Alissa's ear. Onlookers chuckled. Even Lia had to smile. But not Alissa.

Finally the jester shrugged and went on his way to find someone easier to please.

Alissa was close to tears. She turned to Lia. "I give up," she said in a low voice. "I haven't found any answers. And it's too late now to do anything."

She rose and headed for her chambers.

Hours later Alissa was still awake. I'm no closer to solving the riddle than I was at the beginning, she thought.

But as Alissa tossed and turned, an answer came to her. She sat up in bed.

"Oh no," she whispered. "It all fits."

Ever present, yet invisible, she thought. I've lived here all my life, and I'm always present in the castle. But as Balin said, I'm a mouse in the corner. I might as well be invisible.

Unmatched power, but little respect. I'm a princess, so I'm powerful—or will be someday. But since I'm a child, I receive little respect now.

Outside the same, yet inside different. I look the same as I did just a month ago. But, oh, she thought, how different I feel inside!

"*I* am the danger to Arcadia!" Alissa exclaimed. "I'll make a mistake tomorrow, and the alliance will be ruined."

It was a long time before she finally fell into an uneasy sleep.

The Banquet

"Ouch," cried Alissa. "That hurts!"

"I'm sorry, milady," said the serving maid. "But your hair is horribly tangled."

"That's what comes from racing about," said Great-aunt Matilda.

"Racing about," repeated Great-aunt Maude. She looked around blankly as if wondering exactly who might be racing about. And where.

The bedchamber was crowded with people helping Alissa prepare for the banquet. One serving maid was taking last-minute tucks in Alissa's new dress. Others were laying out the rest of the princess's clothing. And the great-aunts were directing everyone and everything.

Alissa wished they would all go away and leave her alone. All but Lia.

At last it was time to put on the gown. Alissa stood in the center of the room. A serving maid slipped the dress over her head.

"Oh, princess, it's beautiful," sighed one of the maids.

"Just beautiful," breathed Lia.

Alissa glanced down. Soft silk flowed in a rich stream to the floor. Beautiful gold threads crisscrossed the top. And over her shoulders, she wore a deep blue robe of thick velvet. It was

70

the loveliest outfit she had ever owned.

She looked over at Lia. The dark green of her friend's dress made her eyes sparkle. And atop her pretty braids, Lia wore a circlet of flowers.

Then Matilda reached into a bag she wore at her waist. "Here," she said. "It's time you had this." She pulled out a crystal necklace.

"This was your mother's," Matilda said gruffly. "And I think she would want you to wear it today." She placed the necklace around Alissa's neck.

The crystal felt cool against Alissa's skin. She looked up at her great-aunt and smiled.

"Thank you," she said softly.

Lia added the last touch by placing a glittering crown on Alissa's head.

"I guess I'm ready now," said the princess.

Alissa headed out the door. Slowly and carefully, she made her way down the stone steps. The hallway below was crowded with royal guests. And they were all watching her.

Then she caught sight of Cook. The big woman was half-hidden at the back of the crowd. A broad smile lit up her face. And then Cook winked. Alissa knew it wasn't entirely proper, but she couldn't help winking back.

As Alissa reached the bottom of the stairs, her father moved forward. His eyes shone with pride. He took her hand and led her toward the king of Thalia.

Roderick bowed. "Princess Alissa," he said. "It is an honor to be your dinner partner."

Alissa took Roderick's arm. Together they followed King Edmund into the great hall. Behind them came the other kings and queens who were honored guests.

The royal party made its way to a table at the side of the hall. Elsewhere, people stood at long tables, silently waiting to be seated.

As she passed through the hall, Alissa noticed how fine things looked. Richly embroidered cloths covered the tables. Instead of the usual bread trenchers, golden plates were set at each place. Never before had such a banquet been served in Arcadia.

At last they reached their chairs. King Edmund was to sit at one end, Alissa at the other. The royal guests would sit along the sides. And Roderick was placed to Alissa's right, in the position of honor.

King Edmund motioned to the guests, inviting them to sit and eat. Everyone started to talk as they took their places. Nervously Alissa eased herself into her chair. The banquet had begun.

Servants brought dish after dish to the tables. Alissa tried to remember everything the great-aunts had taught her.

"Would you care for salt, my lord?" she asked after serving King Roderick a slab of beef. She remembered to sprinkle the salt carefully.

"Something more to drink, sire?" she inquired. She stopped a passing servant and held out the goblet she shared with Roderick.

Meanwhile, she tried to talk with the king. To her surprise, she found Roderick interesting and funny—not cross at all.

Alissa had been sure she wouldn't be able to eat a bite at the banquet. But now she realized that she was hungry. Remembering to use her finest manners, the princess began to eat. She reached out and speared a piece of meat with her knife. Just then King Roderick turned to ask her a question.

Alissa was startled. Her hand slipped. The knife slid across her plate, and a piece of meat skidded away. She watched it tumble right off her plate, right off the table. And right into King Roderick's lap.

Alissa stared at the king's now spotted robe. In terror, she waited for Roderick to rise to his feet. Soon he would be shouting, telling everyone how rude she'd been. Tears filled her eyes.

But nothing happened. Slowly Alissa lifted her head. She caught sight of King Roderick. Much to her surprise, he was smiling!

The king flicked the piece of meat onto the floor. A castle dog grabbed it up.

"She'll thank you for that treat," said the king.

"Oh, your majesty!" Alissa cried. "I-I-I apologize. I didn't mean to do it!"

The king chuckled. "Why, princess, this reminds me of a royal banquet I attended as a boy. I spilled an entire goblet of wine in the lap of a crabby old knight."

He smiled. "It was a very large lap too." His smile got bigger. "And I must be honest. I was secretly glad he had to leave the table to dry himself. He was terribly boring."

He looked at Alissa. "I trust you're not trying to get rid of me? I'm sure you've heard that I am considered somewhat hard to please."

"Oh no, sire," Alissa began. She stopped when she saw the twinkle in his eyes. She smiled back. "Well, I have heard that. And you may have heard things about me as well."

The king laughed. "Let us set all that aside, princess. For I am finding you a most enjoyable dinner partner."

"And I you, sire," said Alissa.

And she was. In fact, Alissa soon stopped thinking about how to do things exactly right. She found her manners didn't get any worse when she stopped worrying. Before long she was deep in conversation with King Roderick. She asked questions about his castle and family. He asked about her lessons and Arcadia's hunting dogs.

As the banquet drew to a close, Roderick rose to his feet. "I should like to make a toast," he announced.

"King Edmund and Princess Alissa," said Roderick. "It is an honor to join you on this occasion. To be honest, I expected a cold welcome in Arcadia. Instead, I have found my hosts to be kind, courteous, and generous."

King Roderick continued. "I came here knowing this alliance was a necessary thing. I shall return feeling that it is also a very good one. Let us drink to peace."

"To peace!" echoed King Edmund and the others. They drank. Then Roderick lifted his cup. Alissa remembered to lower hers—as was the custom in Thalia. King Roderick noticed and smiled at her.

Then trumpets sounded from all corners of the great hall. The Ceremony of Alliance was about to begin.

CHAPTER ELEVEN

A Toast to the Alliance

ing Edmund stood and moved down to the other end of the table. Silently he offered his hand to Alissa. She rose too. Together they made their way to their thrones at the front of the hall.

Alissa noted that the servants had prepared everything for the ceremony while the guests dined. Now a long table stood before the thrones. Golden goblets were lined up at both ends. And in the middle lay the Treaty of Alliance.

As Alissa sat down on her throne, she thought about how strange she felt. For the first time, she began to understand what it would be like to be queen. And she realized that she found the idea exciting.

The other kings and queens seated themselves in front of the table. As the last one settled in place, King Edmund began to speak.

"Today is a great day for Arcadia and its friends," he said. "For we are joining together in peace."

As her father spoke, Alissa looked out at the crowded hall. She had to remind herself that a proper princess would never peer around curiously. So she studied the room as best she could without turning her head.

Except for her father's voice, the hall was silent. Even the acrobats, minstrels, and jesters were quiet. Alissa noticed that some of them had moved as close as possible to the table. Everyone cares about this treaty, she thought. And if not for my father, it wouldn't have happened.

King Edmund finished his speech. He stepped down from the throne and moved to the table. There he signed his name to the treaty. A cheer went up from the crowd.

The king smiled. Then he poured some wine into a goblet and lifted the cup. "I, King Edmund of Arcadia, pledge my loyalty to the alliance," he said. He took a swallow of wine.

Alissa rose and moved forward. Her father passed his cup to her. Alissa's hand shook a little as she took it from him.

"And I, Princess Alissa of Arcadia, pledge my loyalty to the alliance," she said. To her surprise, her words sounded strong and firm.

Alissa took a sip from the goblet. Then she stepped back and sat down. She balanced the goblet carefully on the arm of her throne.

The other kings and queens followed her. One by one, they came forward and signed. And each drank and pledged loyalty to the alliance.

Meanwhile, Alissa watched the crowd for signs of danger. Sir Damon, the dark knight, looked as cross as ever. But she noticed that he hadn't even worn his sword tonight. Balin was right about him, Alissa thought.

And Lady Gwynne—where was she? Alissa spotted the lady in a far corner. Beneath the shelter of her veil, she dabbed at her eyes with a lacy handkerchief.

As Alissa looked around, the words of the riddle twisted and turned in her head. No new ideas came to her.

An excited buzz from the crowd brought Alissa's thoughts back to the ceremony. She realized that it was time for King Roderick to sign the treaty.

A sudden motion caught her eye. But it was just the Thalian jester. He was coming closer to watch his king sign the treaty.

The jester didn't seem to be looking where he was going, however. He bumped against a servant and stumbled into the table. The last goblet tumbled to the floor.

Quickly the jester picked up the cup and returned it to the table. With a red face, he bowed to the kings and queens.

Hardly anyone noticed the accident. For all eyes were turned toward King Roderick. The trumpets sounded again, and the Thalian king stepped forward.

The room hushed as Roderick bent down to add his name to the treaty. Then King Edmund filled the last goblet. Roderick smiled warmly as he took the cup.

"I, King Roderick of Thalia, pledge my loyalty to the alliance," he said in ringing tones. "And to you, King Edmund and Princess Alissa." He turned and looked at all the other rulers. "And to you, my friends. Separately we are weak. But together we are mighty."

Alissa glanced back to the crowd. Everyone was so silent. No one moved. Except—

Her eyes darted to the jester. He seemed to be stuffing something into a bag at his waist. For just a moment, she saw the object clearly. He was holding a goblet like those the kings and queens had used. How could he have such a cup? There were only enough for those who signed the treaty! King Roderick had the last one.

Fear struck Alissa. She leaned forward to stare at King Roderick's goblet. His wine was not the usual deep purple color. It looked greenish gray. And it was bubbling!

No one else seemed to notice. Her father's eyes were on Roderick. And Roderick's were on her father.

Roderick finished his speech and lifted his cup. In a flash, the pieces of the riddle fell into place for Alissa.

Ever present, yet invisible. The jester! He was everywhere. But no one paid him any attention. He was just a clown, after all.

Unmatched power, but little respect. Few had more power than a jester, who could make fun of even the king. Yet few received less respect than one called a "fool."

Outside the same, yet inside different. Roderick's cup looked like all the others. But inside—inside, his was different.

Alissa knew what that difference had to mean. The jester had switched Roderick's cup with another—a poisoned cup. If Roderick drank from it, he would die. And her father, who'd filled the goblet, would surely be blamed. The alliance would be shattered.

Alissa jumped to her feet. "Stop!" she screamed.

CHAPTER TWELVE

The Crystal Clears

lissa raced toward King Roderick and knocked the goblet from his hand. With a loud clang, the cup fell to the floor.

At once the hall was filled with noise and confusion. The Thalian guards drew their swords and surrounded their king. The Arcadian guards did the same for Edmund.

Great-aunt Maude quietly fainted and slid off her seat. Matilda reached down and patted her sister's hand. Lia tried to make her way through the crowd to Alissa. And the jester began to slip away toward the entrance to the great hall.

Alissa darted forward again. "Stop him!" she called.

But as Alissa started after the jester herself, a Thalian guard roughly gripped her arm. And over the guard's head, she could see the face of King Roderick. He was staring at her in disbelief.

An Arcadian guard raised his sword. "Take your hands from the princess," he ordered.

"Your princess has insulted the king," snarled the Thalian guard. "And in so doing, she has insulted all of Thalia." However, he let go of Alissa.

Alissa looked around wildly. To her relief, another guard had grabbed the jester. But the jester was laughing and pointing at her. And the guard looked like he was about to let the jester go.

"Enough!" roared King Edmund. He pushed through his guards and made his way to Alissa's side. Placing his hand on her shoulder, he spoke to King Roderick.

"My daughter does not act without thought and reason," he said. "Let her explain herself."

King Roderick studied Alissa's face for a moment. "Put away your swords," he told his guards. He pushed past them and stepped forward.

"King Edmund is right," he said. "I will hear Princess Alissa's story."

Alissa glanced at the jester to make sure that he was still under guard. Then she looked directly at King Roderick.

"Sire," she began, "I beg your pardon. But I acted out of fear for your life."

Gasps and cries flew through the crowd.

"And why did you fear for my life, princess?" asked Roderick calmly.

"I had reason to think that your goblet was poisoned," said Alissa. "And I was afraid that if you drank from it, you would die."

Another murmur ran through the crowd. Alissa paid no attention.

"I noticed the jester putting a goblet into his bag. I knew there were only enough cups to go around. That meant the jester must have switched one cup for another. Then I looked at the goblet in your hand. And I could see that your wine looked strange."

Alissa took a deep breath. "Sire, I know I'm sometimes quick to jump to conclusions. I may be wrong in my thinking. But I didn't dare wait."

As she finished, a Thalian guard bent down. He reached

for the goblet, which had rolled under the table.

"Don't touch it!" cried King Roderick.

Everyone watched in horror as the golden goblet melted into a smoking puddle of metal.

King Edmund turned to his guards. "Search the jester!" he ordered. Arcadian soldiers quickly surrounded the jester. From the bag at his waist, they pulled another golden goblet.

King Roderick's eyes went from the smoking metal to the stolen goblet and back to Alissa.

"It appears that you were right," he said. He took Alissa's hands in his own. "You are a remarkable young woman, Alissa. You feared for my life more than you did for your own. You know that my guards might have harmed you."

"I didn't think that far ahead," admitted Alissa.

"You've saved the alliance," said Roderick gratefully. "And my life. I am your servant." He bowed to her.

Alissa was startled. A king was actually calling himself her servant!

Alissa curtsied. "And I am yours, my lord," she said.

Roderick turned to King Edmund. "Shall we get on with the ceremony?" he asked. "If someone could spare me a cup…"

King Edmund nodded. "Alissa, King Roderick's goblet seems to have ended up in the wrong hands. Perhaps you might offer him a drink from your own."

Alissa curtsied once again. She picked up her goblet and offered it to the Thalian king.

Roderick accepted the goblet with a smile. "I, King

Roderick of Thalia, pledge my loyalty to the alliance," he said loudly. He lifted the cup to his lips and drank.

Then, turning to the crowded room, he raised the goblet high into the air. "To the alliance!" he shouted.

"To the alliance!" echoed the crowd.

King Edmund nodded to the guard who held the jester. "Take that villain to the dungeon," he ordered. "We'll deal with him later."

Then he offered his arm to Alissa. As he led her back to her throne, he bent down to whisper. "Well done, Alissa. And very brave."

Everyone took their places for the concluding words. Though it was hard to settle down again, the ceremony had to be finished. Sir Drear started a long, dull speech about what he called "the poetry of alliance."

Alissa tried to pay attention. But she kept thinking of Balin. The wizard's warnings had really saved the alliance. He should be told that all was now well.

Alissa glanced around. Sir Drear's wandering speech had put many guests to sleep. She whispered an excuse to her father and left the room. No one seemed to notice.

As the princess entered the hallway, she heard some shouts.

"Oh no!" Alissa breathed. The racket was coming from the dungeon stairway.

A guard appeared at the top of the stairs. "He escaped!" the guard shouted. "The jester escaped!"

Two more guards ran past Alissa, swords drawn. She heard the first guard call to them. "One minute he was there!" the guard was saying. "And the next he was gone!"

The three guards hurried back down the stairway. Alissa

wondered whether she should get her father. But then she heard a soft voice calling her name. The sound seemed to come from the far end of the hall.

Balin stepped out of the darkness, wrapped in a deep black cloak. On his shoulder was Bartok—silent for once.

"Balin!" Alissa cried. She hurried to his side. "What are you doing here?" The old wizard never appeared in the main part of the castle.

Without waiting for his reply, she raced ahead. "I was just coming to see you. To tell you what happened."

Balin stepped closer. "I know what happened," he said. "The crystal suddenly cleared, and I could see everything. The cup flying from King Roderick's hand. The guard holding you. The jester sneaking away. I hurried here as fast as I could."

"The spell must have been broken when I knocked the cup aside," said Alissa.

"Yes, Alissa. You broke the spell," said Balin. "Now tell me how you solved the riddle."

Quickly the princess explained how she'd finally put all the pieces together.

"Excellent, excellent," said the old wizard. "You used your powers of thought and observation well, as I knew you would."

"But there are still mysteries," said Alissa. "For one thing, how could a jester have such power? And how could he have vanished?"

"Ah," said Balin with a knowing nod. "When the crystal cleared, I could see the traitor's true identity. And I fear they will not catch the villain. The jester is not a jester, but an old enemy of mine. One who can take many forms."

"Who?" breathed Alissa.

"A sorcerer," said Balin. "A sorcerer who uses his powers for evil. And he is very clever."

Then the wizard smiled at Alissa. "Though not as clever as he thought," he said. "He was able to remain hidden from me. But not from my clever student."

"Clever, clever!" squawked Bartok.

Alissa laughed. "Why, Bartok, that's the first nice thing you've ever said to me."

Balin laughed too. Then he grasped Alissa's hand in farewell. "Now you must return to the ceremony," he said. "You've earned your place there. Besides, listening to Sir Drear will give you another chance to practice patience."

With that, the old man stepped back into a corner. As Alissa watched, his figure blended into the deep shadows.

"Alissa!"

Alissa turned and saw her father approaching.

"Father," she cried as she ran to him. "Have you heard about the jester's escape?"

King Edmund frowned. "Yes, Alissa. I was just returning from a talk with the guards. And…"

He glanced down the hallway, a puzzled look on his face.

"What's the matter?" asked Alissa.

"I was sure I heard you talking to someone," said the king. "And then I thought I saw someone I once knew."

He shook his head. "But it couldn't be. He never goes out these days. Never. It couldn't be him."

"Couldn't be whom?" asked Alissa. She waited for her father's answer. Perhaps Balin was wrong about something after all. Perhaps her father *did* remember the wizard.

"An old man I knew when I was a boy," King Edmund

replied. "A fussy old man who was always giving me long, dry lessons. Then he would send me out on hair-raising adventures. 'Quests,' he called them."

The king laughed. "He always thought he was right. I guess when I think about it, he always *was* right. In fact, he taught me a lot about how to be a king."

Suddenly King Edmund fell silent. He peered closely at Alissa. Then he glanced down the dark hallway again.

Alissa held her breath.

"It seems that some things never change," her father said gently. "I suspect that someone is now teaching you the same lessons." He smiled.

And Alissa smiled back.

Together, king and princess returned to the ceremony.

More to Explore

Have fun exploring about medieval banquets and treats. And there are great projects for you to do too!

Edible Stained Glass

During the later part of the Middle Ages, some castles and churches were built with windows of stained glass. Lovely scenes were created using different colors of glass. The pieces were held together in lead frames.

You can create stained glass designs of your own. But you can eat yours—because your glass will be candy. And your frames will be sugar cookies! Be sure to get permission to use the oven, or ask an adult to help you.

What you need

- Batch of sugar cookie dough. Use a commercial cookie mix, a package of refrigerated cookie dough, or a batch from your favorite recipe.
- Rolling pin
- Cutting board or pastry cloth
- Cookie cutters or table knife
- Two cookie sheets
- Two rolls of assorted Lifesavers® candy
- Turner

What you do

1. Preheat the oven to the temperature recommended on the package or in the cookbook.

2. On a cutting board or pastry cloth, roll out the dough to a thickness of ½". Use cookie cutters or a knife to make shapes.

3. Use smaller cookie cutters or a knife to cut out sections in the middle of the shapes. Make sure your cutouts are about twice as big as a Lifesavers® candy. (As it bakes, the dough will puff up and fill in the spaces a bit.)

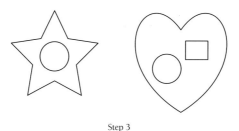

Step 3

4. Carefully lift the shapes and place them on a greased cookie sheet. (Grease the cookie sheets with solid shortening—even if the cookie directions say not to.) Leave about 1" of space between cookies. Then put one candy in the middle of each cutout. (Or two candies if the opening is large enough.)

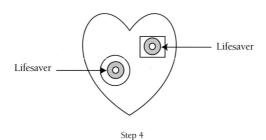

Step 4

5. Continue until the cookie sheet is full. Then bake the cookies according to the package or recipe directions. The candy will melt and fill the cut-out spaces. While the cookies are baking, use the rest of the dough to fill the second cookie sheet.

6. When cookies are done, allow them to cool on the cookie sheet for about two minutes. Then use a turner to carefully remove them.

Banquet Business

What if you were invited to a real medieval banquet? Would you know what to expect? Read on to find out.

How should you behave?

Think about the table manners you've been taught. Then read the list below. It describes a few of the rules that you'll be expected to follow.

- Wash your hands before eating.
- Don't put your elbows on the table.
- Keep your fingernails clean.
- Don't burp at the dinner table.
- Don't put too much into your mouth at once.

Those guidelines probably all sound familiar. But these might be new to you.

- Never dip more than three fingers into the stewpot.
- Don't throw bones back into the pot—throw them on the floor.
- Never wipe your mouth on the tablecloth.
- Don't dip your meat into the salt bowl.
- Wipe your spoon and knife after you use them.
- Wipe your mouth before drinking.
- Don't spit on the table—or over it!

Though you might wonder about some of these rules, there's a good reason behind most of them.

At the banquet, you'll use your hands to take food from the serving dishes. And though you'll cut food with a knife, you'll eat with your fingers. (Forks were very rare in medieval times.)

91

That's why it's important to have clean hands and fingernails.

You'll probably share a cup and silverware with your dinner partner. So it's polite to wipe them off after you use them.

As for throwing the bones on the floor, it's not being messy. The castle dogs are standing by to enjoy any scraps or bones that diners drop.

What will the banquet be like?

The banquet will be held in a great hall and will probably begin around 10 AM. The stone floors will be covered with straw or woven reed mats. Diners will take their places at long tables and benches set up by servants.

You'll need to know where to sit. The most important people sit at a table that's higher than the others. That way they can look out—and down—at everyone else.

Places will be set for you and the other guests. You may see knives and spoons, dishes of salt, silver goblets, and shallow wooden bowls.

But you won't see any plates. Instead, there will be a thick slice of stale bread for you and your dinner partner to share. It's called a *trencher* and it's where you put your meat. If you're still hungry at the end of the meal, you can eat your trencher. If not, you can throw it to the dogs or give it to the poor.

Before your food comes, a horn will blow. That's the signal to wash your hands. Servants will bring pitchers of water, washing bowls, and towels. Don't forget your fingernails!

At last it's time to eat. A parade of servants will carry in the food. First come bread and butter. Next wine and ale. Then the rest of the feast arrives. You might have fish, beef, stuffed boar or pig, and venison (deer). And almost any kind of bird—from pigeons and pheasants to swans and peacocks—might be on the menu.

You'll have lots of other things to eat as well. Pies and cakes will be served at the same time as the meat. You'll see honey and fruit too. So you don't have to wait until the end of the feast for dessert.

Between courses the servants may bring out a dish called a *subtlety*. This is a fancy sculpture made from sugar paste. The subtlety might be in the shape of a castle, a swan, or even the lord of the manor!

Throughout the meal, you'll be entertained. Minstrels will stroll the hall, singing and strumming their lutes. Jesters will go from table to table, trying to make guests laugh. There might even be a storyteller or two.

After the meal ends, it's time to clear things away. That includes the tables and benches. For at night, the great hall sometimes becomes a huge bedroom. And the guests sleep on the floor!

Sugar Castle

As you now know, a medieval banquet could be a huge feast. You may not want to eat like a medieval lord, but here's a fun banquet idea. Make a subtlety of your own—a castle of sugar. But remember: Your castle is to look at, not to eat!

What you need

- Thick cardboard (at least 9" x 12")
- Two one-pound boxes of sugar cubes
- White glue
- Piece of thin cardboard (not corrugated; a shoebox lid is ideal)
- Ruler
- Scissors
- Toothpick
- Colored paper
- Markers

What you do

These directions are suggestions only. You can make your castle bigger, smaller, with more towers—however you want!

1. Place the thick cardboard on a flat surface. This will be the base of your castle.

2. Lay the first row of sugar-cube "stones" for the outside walls of the castle. You will be adding a tower later, so start the wall a bit left of center. Make the back wall nine cubes long and the side walls five cubes long. But be sure to leave a one-cube wide opening in the front wall for the castle entrance. Add a dab of glue to the bottom and one side of each cube as you put it in place.

94

3. Glue four more layers of sugar cubes in place to make walls five cubes high.

4. At each side of the door opening, glue a stack of three cubes to the front wall.

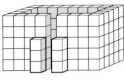

Step 4

5. Cut a thin piece of cardboard 1½" x ⅜". Glue this in place across the top of the two stacks you made at the sides of the door.

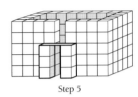

Step 5

6. Cut a thin piece of cardboard 4½" x 3". Glue this in place across the top of the walls of the castle.

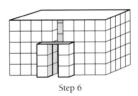

Step 6

7. Cover the castle roof completely with a layer of sugar cubes. Then glue one more row of cubes along the outside edge of this layer. (This way, the wall will rise above the roof of the castle.)

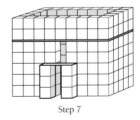

Step 7

8. Glue a sugar cube in every other space around the top layer of the castle walls. Add four layers of sugar cubes, in the pattern shown, to the top of the castle door opening.

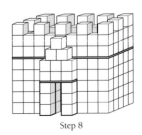

Step 8

95

9. Create a tower at the right side of the castle. Starting about 1" in front of the castle walls, make a square three cubes on each side. Build it ten cubes high. Finish the tower off by gluing a sugar cube to each corner.

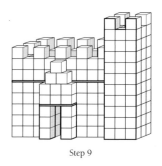

Step 9

10. Add the finishing touches. If you want, you can carefully color a few cubes with black or dark blue marker to show windows. Then make a banner to fly from the castle tower. Cut a piece of colored paper in the shape shown at the right. Cover the wrong side with glue. Then place a toothpick in the middle of the shape, along the fold line. Fold and hold until the glue dries. Put a little glue on the end of the toothpick and stick it down between two cubes on the tower.

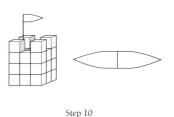

Step 10

11. Now finish the area around the castle. You can glue down blue paper to create a moat. Then make a drawbridge out of brown paper to go across the moat. To make fields, use the brown paper again and stripe it with green marker. You can also cut bushes and trees from the green and brown paper and glue them in place. If you like, add a moat monster too!

Stardust Story Sampler

Stardust Classics books feature other heroines to believe in. Come explore with Laurel the Woodfairy and Kat the Time Explorer. Here are short selections from their books.

Selection from

LAUREL THE WOODFAIRY

"It's no use!" cried Laurel. "I just can't play this tune!"

Laurel lowered her flute. Her beautiful fairy wings drooped as she thought about the long hours she'd spent practicing.

"I'll never be ready for the Celebration of the Chronicles. All the other woodfairies will have some wonderful poem or picture or dance to share. But I won't have a thing to contribute."

Her contribution to the Celebration had to be just right. It should capture the beauty and peace of the woods.

"Please let my tune do honor to the Celebration," Laurel whispered. She left the clearing and headed for her own home.

Laurel had chosen to build her house high in the upper branches of a huge oak. Most fairies liked to live near the ground. But Laurel loved being close to the breeze, birds, and sunbeams.

Laurel's heart lifted as she entered her cheerful home. She placed her bag on a shelf, then picked up her journal. "Maybe I'll take my journal down to the waterfall," she said softly.

She put her cloak back on and glided to the ground. After settling on a rock near the pond, she began to write.

A sudden movement at the edge of the pond caught

Laurel's attention. A tiny head poked through the long grass. It was her friend Mistletoe the mouse.

Laurel got down off the rock and stretched out on the grass. She propped her chin on her hands so that she was face-to-face with Mistletoe. "Hello!" she said. "What have you been up to lately?"

Mistletoe wiggled her nose. "I went exploring all the way to the edge of the Dappled Woods."

"How exciting!" said Laurel. Like all other fairies, Laurel had never been outside the Dappled Woods.

Mistletoe nervously scratched her ear. "I don't know," she said. "Something seemed wrong."

As Mistletoe spoke, Chitters the chipmunk joined them. Chitters was another of Laurel's animal friends. Now he twitched his furry tail and asked what was going on.

"Mistletoe is worried that something's wrong in the Great Forest," Laurel reported.

Chitters flicked his ears. "Worry, worry. No point in it, I say."

"Mistletoe doesn't worry without a good reason," began Laurel. But she was interrupted by the mouse.

"Listen!" Mistletoe squeaked.

Then they heard it. An unfamiliar noise in the bushes behind them.

Mistletoe sniffed the air wildly. "A stranger!" she exclaimed. "Hide!"

At once the two animals disappeared into the brush.

"A stranger?" Laurel questioned. "But—"

Before she could say another word, someone bumped hard against her. Whoever-it-was tumbled to the ground with a thud.

Laurel jumped to her feet. Someone had tripped over her! She'd never heard of a fairy who tripped over other fairies before! Except maybe for herself.

Then she noticed something very odd about the other fairy's back. She had no wings! This wasn't a fairy at all!

Selection from

KAT THE TIME EXPLORER

Kat sighed. There had to be some secret to the time machine. She and Jessie had gotten it put together. Now if they could just get it to work!

Slowly and carefully, Kat ran her hands over the surface of the machine. Inch by inch, her fingers pressed and prodded.

Kat was pressing on the left side of the machine when it happened. There was a tiny movement beneath her fingers.

"Jessie!" Kat cried. "I've found something!"

Jessie hurried over. While her aunt watched, Kat slid open a small, thin drawer.

"It's a secret compartment," said Kat. "You have to know just where to push!"

"What can it be for?" asked Jessie in excitement. "There's nothing in there."

"But look at the bottom of the drawer," said Kat. "See those hollow round spaces? I bet the medallions we found fit there!"

Quickly Jessie got the two medallions. Kat watched as her aunt popped them into place, chains and all.

Nothing happened. Then Jessie slid the drawer back into

the machine. Nothing.

"Well, they fit," said Jessie. "But they don't seem to do anything."

"I was hoping that they might be the power source for the machine," said Kat.

"It doesn't look like it," commented Jessie. "Still, let me check the notebook one more time. Perhaps I missed some clue about what they're for."

While Jessie paged through the notebook, Kat experimented with the medallions. "Maybe they have to go in another way," she whispered to herself.

First she put the silver one where the gold one had been. Then she flipped them over. Nothing happened.

Kat kept trying until there was only one possibility left. She placed the silver medallion on the right—with the front showing. She set the gold medallion on the left—with the back showing.

At once a strange humming sound filled the room!

"What's going on?" called Jessie. She jumped to her feet and started across the room. Grabbing the other end of the machine, she shouted, "Let go, Kat!"

But before Kat could move, a ray of sunlight shone through the small basement window. The light poured over the time machine and lit up the open drawer. The medallions began to glow. Swirling ribbons of mist rose up around Kat and Jessie.

In a matter of seconds, the basement lab faded from sight. Kat couldn't see or hear Jessie.

Suddenly a whistle screamed and the ground began to shake. Kat gazed about blindly, trying to make sense of it all. Where was she? And where was Jessie?

Just as she was about to shout Jessie's name, the mist parted. To her relief, Kat saw her aunt standing across from her. But nothing else was familiar. The basement lab had vanished. Now they stood in the corner of a huge, domed building. People were rushing in every direction. And beside Kat and Jessie was a wall of gleaming black iron.

"It's a train!" cried Jessie. "An old-fashioned steam loco-motive!"

As they watched, the train slowly inched forward. It came to a stop farther down the platform, hissing and spitting like a great dragon.

"What happened?" gasped Kat.

"It worked, Kat!" Jessie answered. "I don't know how, but it did!"

"We've really gone back into the past," whispered Kat.